THE SOCIAL AFFAIR

BRITNEY KING

WWW.BRITNEYKING.COM

ALSO BY BRITNEY KING

Speak of the Devil

The Replacement Wife

Water Under The Bridge

Dead In The Water

Come Hell or High Water

Bedrock

Breaking Bedrock

Beyond Bedrock

Around The Bend

Somewhere With You

Anywhere With You

THE SOCIAL AFFAIR

BRITNEY KING

.

COPYRIGHT

Hot Banana Press

Cover Design by Britney King LLC

Cover Image by Mario Azzi

Copy Editing by Librum Artis Editorial Services

Proofread by Proofreading by the Page

First Edition: 2018

ISBN 13: 978-1979057455

ISBN 10: 1979057451

britneyking.com

To those who've walked into our lives without first asking permission...

PROLOGUE

A ttachment is an awfully hard thing to break. I should know. I surface from the depths of sleep to complete and utter darkness. I don't want to open my eyes. I have to. "I warned you, and I warned you," I hear his voice say. It's not the first time. He called out to me, speaking from the edge of consciousness, back when I thought this all might have been a dream. It's too late for wishful thinking now. This is his angry voice, the one I best try to avoid. My mind places it immediately. This one is reserved for special occasions, the worst of times.

I hear water running in the background. Or at least I think I do. For my sake, I hope I'm wrong. I try to recall what I was doing before, but this isn't that kind of sleep. It's the heavy kind, the kind you wake from and hardly know what year you're in, much less anything else. I consider how much time might have passed since I dozed off. Then it hits me.

"You really shouldn't have done that," he says, and his eyes come into focus. Those eyes, there's so much history in them; it's all still there now. I see it reflected back to me. I read a quote once that said... a true mark of maturity is when someone hurts you, and you try to understand their situation instead of trying to hurt them back. This seems idealistic now. I wish someone had warned me. Enough of that kind of thinking will get you killed.

"Please," I murmur, but the rest of what I want to say won't come. It's probably better this way. I glance toward the door, thinking about what's at stake if I don't make it out of here alive, wondering whether or not I can make a break for it. It's so dark out—a clear night, a moonless sky. The power is out, I gather, and it's a fair assumption. This has always been one of his favorite ways to show me what true suffering is like. That alone would make an escape difficult. I would have to set out on foot and then where would I go? Who would believe me?

"You have it too easy," he says, as though he wants to confirm my suspicions. "That's the problem nowadays. People consume everything, appreciate nothing."

He lifts me by the hair and drags me across the bedroom. I don't have to ask why. He doesn't like to argue where he sleeps, where we make love. It's one of our safe spaces, but like many things, this too is a facade. Nothing with him is safe.

"You like your comforts, but you forget nothing good comes without sacrifice."

"I haven't forgotten," I assure him, and that much is true. Sacrifice is something I know well.

He shakes his head, careful to exaggerate his movements. He wants the message he sends to sink in. "I don't know why you have to make me so angry."

I glance toward the window, thinking I see headlights, but it's wishful thinking. Then I reach up and touch the wet spot at the crown of my head. I pull my hand away, regretful I felt the need for confirmation. Instinct is enough. If only I'd realized this sooner. I didn't have to put my fingers to it to know there would be blood; the coppery scent fills the air. "It's not too bad," he huffs as he slides one hand under my armpit and hauls me up. "Come on," he presses, his fingertips digging into my skin. "Let's get you stitched up."

I follow his lead. There isn't another option. Head wounds bleed a lot, and someone's going to have to clean his mess up. If I live, that someone will be me. *This is how you stop the bleeding.* "What time is it?"

"Oh," he says, half-chuckling. "There's no need to worry about that. She's already come and gone."

I don't ask who he's referring to. I know. Everything in me sinks to the pit of my stomach. It rests there and I let it. I don't want him to see how deeply I am affected by what he's done. It's more dangerous if I let it show. But what I want to happen and what actually does, are two very different things. I know because my body tenses, as it gives over to emotion until eventually it seizes up completely. I don't mean for it to happen. It has a habit of betraying me, particularly where he is concerned. Your mind may know when something's bad for you. But the body can take a little longer. He knows where to touch me. He knows what to say. Automatic response is powerful, and like I said before, attachment is hard to break.

He shoves me hard into the wall. I guess I wasn't listening. I shouldn't have made a habit of that either. I don't feel the pain. I don't feel anything. "Ah, now look what you made me do," he huffs, running his fingers through his hair. He's staring at me as though this is the first time he's seeing me. His face is twisted. He wants me to think he's trying to work out his next move. He isn't. He's a planner, through and through.

Still, he's good at concealing what he doesn't want anyone to know. If only I'd been more like that. I wasn't. That's why I don't know if this is it, if this is the end. I only know where it began.

"We had an agreement," he reminds me. And he's right.

We did have an agreement.

That's how this all started.

CHAPTER ONE

JOSIE

Two months earlier

The voice comes out of nowhere. I don't have to turn around to know how unfortunate this situation is. The sound is male, all male, hard and rough. Breathless and edgy. "Give me the purse," it demands. I exhale slowly. Steady my breathing. Ball my fists. Release them. Flex my fingers. *Jesus.*

I turn in disbelief, hoping I've heard wrong. The lot was empty, I know. I checked three times. Only it isn't, at least not anymore, because all of a sudden, here I am, staring down the barrel of a gun. A bad sign if there ever was one in regard to how my day might end. The man who holds it is clothed in black. Also not a good sign. He wears a ski mask that doesn't conceal his eyes, and he should know that's where the soul lives. His stance is wide, head tilted, shoulders squared. It's almost comical, save for the gun pointed at my head, like a scene straight out of a movie. He clears his throat. "I said. Give. Me. The. Purse."

I sigh and then I make a move as though I intend to slide it from my shoulder. Thankfully, the universe isn't completely against me—a trash truck, somewhere a block or two over, slams

13

a dumpster back to its rightful place, and for a brief second, his attention is diverted. It helps that he isn't expecting anything other than compliance. I see it in his soul.

I twist myself, position my body for maximum effect, and land a blow to his kneecap. It hits just right, and the direct hit, combined with the element of surprise, sends him down. He drops the gun in favor of his knee; that's where the hands tend to go when you inflict this level of pain from that angle. I know, I learned this where people learn most things these days: on the internet.

I take a few steps toward him, and I pick up the gun. His eyes widen as I take aim. It's a dumb move—I don't even know if it's loaded. I don't know the gun; I don't know important things—like whether the safety is on, what caliber of bullet it holds, or more importantly, what he'd have to do to make me pull the trigger. "Don't move," I order. My voice comes out calm, steadier than I feel. But then, I've had years of practice in that regard.

He puts his hands up, and then drops them so he can scoot backward.

I dig my heel into the pavement, widen my stance. "Take off the mask."

He's slow to move at first, but when I threaten to internet karate chop him again, he gets the message. He removes the mask, and this is how I know the gun is in fact loaded. I smile, thankful I made the right call.

"Better," I say.

"Please," he begs. He holds his palms upward in my direction. He wants to give me the illusion of control, even though he's bigger and stronger and likely faster. I grip the gun tighter. It's nice to have an equalizer. I'm grateful he chose a gun and not a knife because if the latter were the case, I'd have to get closer to him, giving him the advantage in the process. "Please," he says again. "I have a family."

"Most people do."

"I...I—" He begins to squirm. Nerves, I presume. That or he's trying to distract me. Neither are a good choice.

I deliver another kick, this time to the opposite kneecap, just to ensure he doesn't move. Then I fish the Altoid I had been digging for from my pocket and slip it onto my tongue. *One should always come prepared.* He's whimpering, writhing on the ground, shuffling back and forth from his right side to his left. His pained expression makes him look younger than he is. With his curly hair and jet-black eyes, he isn't unattractive. It makes me wonder what would have to happen in a person's life to make it come to this.

Slowly, I take three steps backward. And then one more just to be sure. "It's almost Christmas," I say. "What are you thinking, robbing people at a time like this?"

He looks at me strangely. Christmas means nothing to him. Also, he thinks I'm an idiot. Christmas, or any other time, really— thieves aren't selective— is the perfect time to steal what isn't yours. People are distracted. They let their guards down, all too willing to believe in what's good. I realize this now.

"Do you know what could have happened if I'd given you my purse?"

He furrows his brow and considers my question. He's expecting a sob story. I don't look as desperate as I am. Eventually, his face twists as though I'm crazy, and today he isn't wrong. Finally, he shakes his head.

"I might have wound up dead. That is—if you didn't kill me first."

"I'm sorry," he says. But it's a lie, only as sincere as the predicament in which he's now found himself.

"Give me one reason I shouldn't pull the trigger..."

He doesn't immediately answer me, and this makes me nervous. Every second counts. I've learned this lesson well. "It's not like it wouldn't be self-defense."

"My grandma," he says, finally. Before he starts huffing and hawing about his knees again.

"Your grandma." I tilt my head. I hadn't expected that.

"Yeah, I look after her. She's blind and bedridden."

"What does that have to do with me?"

"If I don't go home, no one will find her. Not for days...."

I reposition the gun, lower it slightly and then raise it again. I look down the barrel and line up the sight. Then I squeeze one eye shut the way they do in the movies. "I don't believe you."

He starts waving his hands. This is his problem in life, I can see. No one taught him how to use words to get what he wants, so he resorts to violence. "She has diabetes. I need the money for insulin."

I study him carefully. He has a sense of desperation about him. And not just because I have a gun pointed at his heart. I read about that on the internet, too. Where to aim. Makes it hard to miss. Anyway, I know the look, and somehow I think he might be telling the truth, which makes this situation all the more sad.

"Fine," I say. "But prison is going to cost you a lot more than insulin." I know as the words leave my mouth what I'm saying isn't altogether true. If he is in fact telling me the truth, not getting the insulin his grandmother needs would have far greater effects than knowing he did what he could and went to jail for it. Either way, he failed. But in his mind, in the latter scenario, at least he would know he'd given it his all. Street credit. That's his currency.

I watch as he shifts onto his side. He's slow and careful about it and still I make sure the gun is trained on him. He reaches into his pocket, and I learn quick— there's no safety. "Make another move and you're dead."

"Wait," he calls out, and it's a piece of paper he's retrieved, not a weapon. "See—it's her prescription."

"Keep your hands where I can see them," I say. It's cliché. I feel it as the words float off into the breeze. *Look how cliché you've become, Josie.* But I have to admit, when your life is at stake, sometimes it's the most logical thing to say.

I take two more steps backward. It surprises him when I throw my purse at him. He ducks and covers his head.

"In the right pocket, there's a hundred-dollar bill. Get it out."

His eyes narrow; he's confused. He reaches for it and pulls it toward him anyway.

"Not that one," I nod. "The small pocket."

He digs. I look up at the sky and notice the big puffy clouds, the kind the kids and I used to spend hours staring at. We imagined they were dragons and dinosaurs, angels and other things too. I wish I could go back. Back to a time when I wasn't where I am now, back against the wall, back to when things were idyllic and stable. Even if it was all a facade. You can't know that you don't want to know a thing until you already know it. Once it's there, you can't erase it. It's interesting; you don't realize how you'll miss stability, predictability even, until the rug is pulled out from under you.

"Got it," he calls out. I hear relief in his tone, and I know I will regret this later. There will be hell to pay. I also know I shouldn't reward a kid who just tried to rob me. But when you're down on your luck, sometimes it's good to know others have it worse. Plus, it would have been really bad if I'd had to explain where I was when I lost my purse. I should count my blessings.

I cock my head. "Slide the purse back."

He does, and I use my foot to inch it closer, keeping the gun on him.

"You almost shot someone's mother. I hope you think about that tonight when you're drifting off to sleep."

He doesn't say anything. I can see he doesn't know what to say.

"Oh—and you're going to want to ice those kneecaps."

"Thank you..." he says, shoving the money in his pocket.

"And by the way, I'm keeping this," I tell him, holding the gun up.

He sighs heavily, and I can see his weapon was hard to come by. This is both bad and good. Good because it shows he won't easily be able to get a replacement. Bad because it tells me he needs one. "Turn around." I use the gun to motion him in the direction I want him to go.

He scoots around, going counter-clockwise. "Don't get up until you no longer hear my engine. Otherwise—I'll turn right back around and hold you here until the cops show up."

"Okay."

I bite my lip. It hits me then. The answer to my questions might very well be right in front of me. *The simplest answer's usually the right one.* "Let me ask you a question..."

He glances over his shoulder.

I tilt my head. "Do you think one has a moral obligation to stop something horrible from happening to another person?"

His eyes narrow. He thinks I'm referring to this situation. He thinks I'm referring to him. "I don't know."

"You know what I think?"

He juts out his bottom lip and shakes his head.

"I think most people would say yes."

He shrugs again. "Sounds very philosophical. Where I come from they don't teach much of that."

"Life teaches you," I say.

He watches me carefully.

"But what if that person wronged them? Does the rule still apply?"

"Rules are rules." He doesn't believe his own lie.

"What about karma? Survival of the fittest?"

"I think karma has a way of working itself out. I don't really think you have to help it along..."

It's the first intelligent thing he's said. But he's wrong. Sometimes you do have to help it along. Alternatively, sometimes, and as luck would have it, in his case, you decide to just let it be.

"Turn around."

He does as I ask. But first, I see the confusion on his face. It's mixed with a bit of terror. He isn't completely convinced I won't put a bullet in the back of his head. It's better this way.

I wait for a second just to make sure he continues to face the opposite direction. When I'm reasonably confident he's going to comply, I remind him one last time. "Stay." I start backward, carefully, meticulously, toward the safety of my car.

He scoffs. He's not used to being told what to do. This is how it all starts. If only parents could press a fast-forward button, if they could see into the future, then this kid might've had a chance. Now, karma is going to work itself out, and in his case, it's just a matter of time.

"Eyes straight ahead," I remind him once I've reached my car. I don't want him getting a look at my license plate. I've scared him. But probably not enough. Retribution can be a bitch. I should know.

That's why I was here in the first place.

CHAPTER TWO

IZZY

Two months before that...

I notice them straight away. Ironically, it's her that catches my eye first. Not because she is the same as the rest of them, but because she is different. I'm serving up my ten-thousandth non-fat, no whip, ridiculous flavored, over-priced latte of the day when I look up and the clouds part. Sunlight comes pouring in, and I swear if I believed in angels, I could hear them singing. As perfect as the two of them might be. She seems to sense that I am looking, and she smiles, almost shyly, although I'd be willing to bet she isn't that shy at all. She meets my eye and then quickly looks away, toward the man standing to her left. I hadn't quite taken him in, but I do then. Maybe this is what makes her different. *She makes others see what she wants them to see.* She meets my eye, and again she smiles. I'm pretty sure I do hear angels this time. Or maybe it's just the Alanis Morissette song screaming at us over the sound system. I straighten my apron. *She sees me.* The others around here— they never do. For them, I'm just a means to an end, someone to dish out their fix. She meets my eye again, briefly, and I can see it's not like that with her.

When she finally gets up to the counter to place her order, I can tell I'm right by the way her hand flies to her throat as she scans the offering. She isn't sure what she wants; she's not a regular like the majority of women on this side of town.

"Can I help you?" I ask, and this time she doesn't look at me. She's staring at the menu, tracing her collarbone lightly with the tips of her perfect fingers, and it's striking how someone so beautiful could be so unsure of herself.

The man looks over at her, waiting for her to speak, much the same way I am. She's someone it seems like the whole world might be waiting on. *He studies her too.* The expression he wears is so intimate it almost causes me to look away. *Almost.* She's wearing a sleeveless, summer dress and sandals, her striking fire-red hair pulled neatly into a ponytail. And not the lazy kind, like a lot of women sport these days. No, not her. She doesn't have a single hair out of place. Although, I'm sure she could pull off the lazy kind if she wanted to.

I grip the towel hanging from my apron and take a deep breath in. *Get it together, Izzy.* I realize then how ridiculous I must look in comparison. Her eyes shift toward the door before settling back on me. His never do. He's still staring at her. I can't remember the last time a man looked at me that way, or rather maybe I do, and it's safe to say it's been a long time. Maybe this is why when he offers to tip extra well, if only I'll make his wife an Americano, which isn't on our menu, I say yes. Or maybe it's the fact that I desperately need the money. Maybe it's because it feeds the rage inside me, the way rich people think they can dole out dollars like breadcrumbs to those of us who are less fortunate in order to get what they want. I need to feed that rage, particularly now; it's the only thing that gets me out of bed most days.

She places her hand on his arm. "It's okay," she says, and her voice is heavenly. I wonder if they have training for that sort of perfection. She smiles at me. She's not dumb. She knows the whole world rests on her next move. "Give me a sec—" she adds with a squeeze of his forearm, and I'd give her forever if I were him. I can't take my eyes off her. Neither can he. I watch as she presses her lips together, and it could be one of the most stunning things I've ever seen. "I'll figure something else out," she says scanning the menu. She doesn't say it condescendingly, the way most women in her position would. When she speaks it's genuine, like she doesn't want to cause any trouble. It doesn't go unnoticed. Not by me— and not by him either. The truth is, big tip or not, rage or no rage, I knew I'd make her that Americano for the simple fact there was no other choice. I wanted to see her happy. She seems like the kind of person who only knows happiness in her core. But there's more, too, more than meets the eye, this I can see. She seems like the kind of woman who demands more of a person. Like your standards raise just by being in her presence. Like she'll make you better by osmosis.

Her husband clears his throat, and it gets my attention. "You heard the girl, Jos—she said she'd do it."

"It's no problem," I admit, and her eyes meet mine.

She offers a faint smile, closes the menu before opening it once again. Patrons behind them are hemming and hawing and that's the thing about this side of town. No one waits for anything.

Then she looks up. "Don't worry," she quips. There's a gleam in her eye when she speaks. "I won't ask for a sandwich, too."

It seems like an odd thing to say, but I understand what she means; we aren't yet serving lunch, and she doesn't care what people think. I take it for what it is: a sign. *She gets me.* She has a dark sense of humor packaged beneath that sunny act; it's clear as day.

I watch the two of them from my periphery as I wait for the espresso to brew. He whispers something in her ear, and she throws her head back and laughs. Her neck stretches all the way, as far as I think it will go, and I can't help myself, I'd like to find out. It's pale and beautiful, elongated and slim. Half of me wants to reach out and choke her; it isn't fair to be that perfect and

23

happy, and the other half wants something else entirely. He leans in closer then, and I can see she's a siren, silently claiming her prey. When he nuzzles her, it's too much—I have to look away. Only I can't. I can't stop watching.

His phone rings, and she gives him a look. He checks the screen and silences the ringer, like any good husband would. Like mine should have done, but didn't.

The machine finishes. I prepare her drink slowly, slower than I normally would, because I can see that a woman like her demands a slow, careful, delicate kind of love. Also, I'm not ready for this encounter to be over. I'm not ready for them to leave. I imagine inserting myself into their lives for all of eternity. I picture Christmases and birthdays together, and then feel outrage that there really are couples like them that exist in the world. I hadn't wanted it to be true, and yet here they are— living, breathing proof that not only am I a failure, but also wrong.

Eventually, the line backs up, and when it reaches the door, I have no choice but to hand the coffee over. When I do, my elbow accidentally bumps the plastic tip jar, knocking it over onto the floor. I watch in slow-motion as the change hits the concrete floor, bouncing around, taking forever to settle. Everyone's eyes are on the money. Mine too, only I rush around the counter to clean up the mess. By the time I get around to the other side, she's already crouched down collecting coins. It's odd seeing her there, picking up nickels and dimes in such a fancy dress. That dress alone probably cost what I make in an entire month. Including gratuity.

I realize as I collect the spare change no one wants that I could never compete with the likes of that. After all, I have a safety pin holding my bra together where the clasp is supposed to be. She has manicured nails and flawless skin. Someone like her would never like someone like me. It brings to mind everything that's wrong in the world, the unfairness of it all. "I've got this," she says glancing up. Instantly, my thoughts turn to Joshua. *I've got this.* My eyes grow wide. "It's okay," she assures me, shuffling coins back into the jar. "Accidents happen."

I barely hear her. I'm slipping, I'm drowning, and she's somewhere far off, her voice too distant to reach me. I know what comes next. The tunnel. I'm sinking, I'm going under, and I'm not sure I'll ever find my way out. It's like I'm Alice, and I'm choosing the rabbit hole when all I really want to do is stay here with her. My palms grow sweaty, my head buzzes, and if there was anything in my stomach, we'd have a bigger issue on our hands.

I can see her mouth moving, she is speaking, and she's speaking to me. But I don't know what she is saying. *Joshua. No. Please.* I blink rapidly. *This is what my life has become; this is what my life will always be.* That's what my doctor says—he says it may never get better, and suddenly I'm paralyzed, unable to move. My vision blurs. I'm fading...I'm going...I'm giving in.

She stands and brushes her hands on her thighs. She calls my name. Her voice is like butter, no— better than butter—*what's better than butter, I hear Josh ask*— and no, it's not like butter. It's pure silk. Izzy, she calls again, and my name on her lips— it's too much. *My name. How does she know my name?*

"Izzy," she says again. Her voice is calm and firm, and this time she comes into focus. Her head is cocked, but her neck is all I see. Her collarbone catches my eye. Smooth and pink, rounded and perfect. She's staring at my name tag, and when I look up, I notice nothing but the concerned look on her face.

It takes a few moments, maybe eternity. But she brings me back. No one could ever do that. Not even Josh. "Sorry," I offer, glancing away. I clear my throat and smooth my shirt, cursing myself for not making more of an effort. "I have low blood sugar."

As I collect myself, her husband hands me the jar. I stare at him for a second. He seems to want to say something, but he doesn't, and I retreat to my rightful position on the other side of the counter. People in line are complaining like I can't hear them, acting impatient and rude at being denied their overpriced coffee bought in bulk and dressed up in fancy, chemical-laced syrup. They're ridiculous, the lot of them; they're everything that's wrong with society today.

But not her. And not him either. They're patient and kind. Everything love should be.

"Here," she tells me, thrusting the Americano in my direction. "Maybe you need this more than I do."

I stare at the coffee in her hand. I don't drink coffee. And I don't have low blood sugar.

"Maybe you should sit down," the man says. "Is there anyone here that could cover for you?"

I shake my head.

"I see," he says, pushing the tip jar further on to the counter. He's making a point. I move it back slightly too. *Better safe than sorry.* His hand brushes mine, and I look up then. His eyes are green, and in them I don't see anything. Not a worry— not a concern—not a care in the world. And all I know is those are the kind of eyes I'd like to have.

I look up at her. She presses her lips together, thanks me for the coffee and starts for the door, before turning back. "It can only get better from here," she smiles, tilting her coffee in my direction. He doesn't say anything; he simply offers a curt nod before placing his hand on the small of her back. I look on as he leads her out the same door they came in. I'm not the only one. I hear the hushed whispers. I don't, however, hear what's being said. It's no matter, anyhow. She doesn't walk back out into the great big world, she glides, taking all of the air in the room with her when she goes.

I count to four and then I go to the window. I watch as they make their way down the sidewalk, away from me. Away from hard work and sacrifice. Just like that, they're gone. Gone as quickly as they came, and I wasn't ready for it to be over yet.

When they disappear from my line of sight, it takes everything in me not to open that door and run down the street, just to catch another glimpse of what true love looks like. Instead, I lay my forehead against the cool glass, exhaling long and slow, before I turn back to the patrons standing in line. I get back to it. I make coffees. I ring people up. I play catch up. But my heart's not in it. Neither is my mind, really. Questions run through my mind; it's a marathon in there. I want to know what you have to do to get a love like that. I want to know how she managed to get him under her spell, and me too, for that matter. I want to know how she does it, how she makes it look so effortless in the process.

I plan to find out. In the meantime, I adjust my apron, which allows me the briefest of moments to reminisce, and then I do the thing I knew I'd do from the moment her eyes met mine. I write the name on his credit card on my palm—Grant Dunn—just in case it slips my mind, even though I know it won't.

CHAPTER THREE

JOSIE

"You know the rules, Jos—."

"I know," I tell him. *Let no man or woman come between what God has created.* I don't tell him I accepted those rules when I was young, pliable, and hopelessly in love. What good would it do? I may no longer be the former but I can't say with absolution that I'm not the latter. "It's just...well, I feel terrible. I shouldn't have talked her into it..."

He looks over at me and smiles. It's the reassuring kind, the kind he's best known for these days.

"But it was your job. You couldn't have known this was going to happen."

I take a deep breath in, and I hold it. He's right. I can't fault him for all of it, even though I desperately want to.

He makes a left turn, hard and fast. I slide across the leather seat, shifting more than I mean to. "I think you're overreacting," he tells me calmly. "I checked the calendar this morning, in preparation, and you're on cycle day 22. So—" he says, patting my knee. "A little emotional upheaval is to be expected."

I clear my throat. Even after all this time, years spent with a person, sharing their bed, sharing a life, sometimes you see a thing coming and sometimes you don't.

"What's done is done, Josie. Premenstrual or not, do I really need to remind you of the agreement?"

Never second guess a decision once it's been made.

"No," I admit "It's just nerves, you know. I hate to think there is more we could be doing."

I watch his jaw tighten, flex, and release. I watch his knuckles go from pink to white as he grips the wheel, and I know that was the wrong thing to say. Lying is a punishable offense under the agreement he's referring to. So I tiptoe around the truth instead. "I'm sure she's in good hands."

"She'll be fine," he says. I study his profile. He doesn't look worried. Maybe I shouldn't, either. "Anyway, it's out of our control at this point. All we can do is pray," he adds, repositioning his hands on the wheel. He stretches his fingers, and then glances toward me. He's looking to see that I'm on board, and on his face I see it. The calm, in-control mask goes up. "And in any case, she probably won't be there long. Once they treat the infection, she'll be good as new."

"I know," I assure him. I know when to give him what he wants.

He stares straight ahead. "Sometimes these things happen..."

"You're right," I reply, not because I necessarily believe him but because I know there's nothing more to be said. My husband has that way about him. He's an expert at letting you know when the conversation is over, without ever having to say so. I don't tell him how guilty I feel over the whole thing. June was—June is—my friend. I mean, not the real kind. It's been a long time since I've had one of those. She's my Sister In God, my mentor, both New Hope terms, but still. She didn't want that surgery. Her husband wanted it. She told me it wouldn't go well. *She knew.* But given our friendship, given that she was my mentor, it was my job to talk her into doing what her husband said. *Checks and balances.*

30

"I'm going to drop you off," Grant informs me, interrupting my thoughts. He says it so casual and cool. Always so cool. "I have to head to the office."

"The office?" I say as though it's some crazy, far-fetched idea.

"Should I pick up dinner on my way home?" he asks, and this is his way of not answering my question directly. He's very skilled at a lot of things, evasion being high on the list.

I shift in my seat. "You're going into work today?" It's a stupid question, one that he's already answered, in typical fashion, by presenting another question. So, I don't know why I asked, or why my voice raises, turns high-pitched and needy, which is exactly why he gives me the side-eye. I take it for what it is, a warning.

I swallow hard. Suddenly, I wish I hadn't opened my mouth. I should have known better. On all fronts. Grant is married to his work, so why I thought he'd take the entire day off is beyond me — I should've assumed. I guess every once in a while it's nice to be surprised.

"Josie—please." He places his hand over mine. "We've had a good morning."

If you consider visiting a friend who might be dying— all the while knowing it might very well be your fault— a good morning, then yes, I guess you're right. I almost say this to him. I feel like the words could glide out into open air, into the space between us, so easily. But I bite them back. I know where that kind of mistake leads, and it's nowhere good. Plus, it won't help anyway. I know he has a full schedule. I know his patients are demanding. "I'm sorry," I say, because I know how much he hates it when I raise my voice. Also, I wouldn't understand what it's like having work that you love. This is what he's thinking. He hasn't said it yet. Sometimes I like to beat him to the punch.

"Dinner?" he reminds me. "Do I need to get dinner?"

"No." I scroll through my phone. Snap a photo of my shoes next to the Porsche logo on the floor mat and post it to Instalook. Caption it with: Love mornings with my man.

31

Scrolling through my feed, I glance up. He likes it when I post on Instalook. Superficiality is his specialty. "I have to pick up Avery from dance at four. Then I plan to head back up to see June. I'll fix something and leave it in the fridge between now and then..."

He frowns. "You won't be home when I arrive?"

I like eighteen photos. Not so different from my own. Fifteen of them are members of the church, the other three, we're trying to recruit.

"Josie."

"Sorry," I say. "The Chick Tribe has had a busy morning..." That's what we call ourselves. It was a joke at first, or at least I think, but somehow it stuck. Anyway, it's good for business, nonetheless. "What did you ask?"

Ordinarily, he'd be annoyed I wasn't listening. But those two words have power. The kind only money and influence bring.

"Will you be home when I get home?"

"I don't know. Depends on how long things take at the hospital..."

He shakes his head. "There's nothing you can do for June, love. It's important you let her rest." He sighs. "And, she needs to not rely so much on you. We need you at home, Jos ."

"I know," I agree. I check the number of likes I received. Shit. I forgot to tag the shoes. Everyone wants to know where they came from. I glance at the bottom of my heel. I can't remember now and then I look over at my husband. "But the kids are getting older, and you'll be working late... so I just figured—"

He holds his hand up to cut me off. "Is it really so much to ask that the first thing I see when I walk through the door is my wife's beautiful face?"

I swallow hard. "No," I say, and suddenly it clicks. The shoes came from Nordstrom's. Last season. I should have thought of that. I can't very well say this. It'll be disappointing to the tribe. "What time should I have dinner ready?"

He nods and gives another of his reassuring smiles. "That sounds perfect," he says which doesn't answer the question at all. He stops at a red light and just when I think he isn't going to say anything further, he does. "I really couldn't live without you, Josie. I know this isn't easy for you...with everything going on right now...but most things in life that are meaningful aren't easy."

I frown. It sounds like he just pulled a random quote out of thin air and inserted it into our conversation. Also, I feel one of his pep talks coming, and I'm not in the mood. Speaking of easy, I know I shouldn't, but I can't help myself. I don't want to hear it, so I throw him a curveball. "Do you think you can pick up James from soccer?"

"What time?" he asks, furrowing his brow. I don't know why he's confused. It's farcical. For the past seven months, our son's practice has ended at the same time everyday.

"5 o'clock," I answer, careful to keep my tone steady. Neutral. Tone is important to my husband. It's written into the manual.

"Sorry. I can't." He shakes his head. "I have a patient at 4:30."

Of course you do, I almost say. I stare out the passenger window and bite my tongue instead.

"How about stopping off for coffee?"

I look over at him. My husband doesn't drink coffee. Which means I usually don't either. But I see it for what it is—a peace offering.

I look over and nod. "That sounds great."

He winks at me, an unspoken gesture that says so much. He looks so boyish behind the wheel, relaxed, the sunlight glinting off his skin. I see the love written in his expression, and it's hard to be angry about the rest of it. It's familiar, this look, a reminder of what was, what has always been. I remember he winked like that on our wedding day, standing at the altar, as though the two of us were in on some sort of secret the rest of the world didn't get.

"It's a good thing he'll be driving in a few weeks..."

"Huh?" Then I get it. He's not thinking about our wedding day. He's thinking about our son.

"James."

"Yes," I agree, although I'm not so sure. I'm not ready to have another thing to worry about.

I see his eyes glance at the clock on the dash. "They grow up so fast, don't they?"

"They do," I reply, and at least that much is true.

WE STOP FOR COFFEE AT A NEW PLACE, OR AT LEAST I THINK IT'S new. Maybe I just never noticed it before. I don't drink coffee anymore, so it's hard to say. In any case, we don't speak much after that. Grant says silence is golden.

At home, he drops me at the door, or rather in the drive. He has to run. I feel that familiar pang, loneliness, or longing, who's to say? It only lasts for a second, because when I walk in the front door there are a dozen long-stemmed pink roses sitting in the foyer. I lean in and inhale the familiar scent, and then I pluck the card, sliding it between my fingers, feeling the weight of the paper. I open it, even though I'm pretty sure I know what it will say. There are only a few variations. *I love you. Always have. Always will. Love, Grant.*

I lean back and snap the photo with my phone. I post it to Instalook with the hashtag #luckiestwifeever .

And I am the luckiest wife ever. If one is to overlook the fact that my husband had his assistant order these, and someone else deliver them, and the fact that he can't be here for me when I really need him. If you forget to consider those things, then yes, it's all true. I roll my shoulders and try to release the weight of this morning. This isn't his fault, the situation with June. Well, not entirely. I shouldn't be so annoyed with him. He is trying. Clearly, he's trying.

I set my phone down and sit on the plush bench in the foyer. It's well-cushioned and pale green. Grant's choice. I know he won't like me sitting on it, having just been at the hospital. He despises germs, which is why I had to practically beg him to let me see June, given the infection. I half-expected he'd say I shouldn't go back up this afternoon. But he didn't.

I crack my neck and open my phone. I check Instalook to see how many "likes" I've gotten. Forty-five in nineteen seconds. Not bad. Still, I sigh. I reply to the comments about the shoes. Grant brought them back for me from a trip, I lie.

I cross and uncross my legs. Smooth my dress. If I lean forward just enough I can see her house. I don't want to, but sometimes it's an itch I have to scratch. I scratch hard this time, allowing myself a good, hard look. It's so different now, so empty without her, even though it isn't empty at all. So much has changed, and yet nothing has. Kate was my best friend. I make myself look away. I thumb through Instalook, see what the Chick Tribe is up to. This helps.

I don't like to think about how good it used to be. That's why I don't look often, not anymore. It hurts too much, even after all this time. But sometimes on occasion, if I'm antsy, the way I am now, I allow myself just a peek, a tiny glimpse into the past. I'm careful though. I don't venture too far down that path or there are consequences. Friends like Kate don't come around often, and in fact, and I know it sounds cliché, but I've never met anyone like her since. I don't think I ever will. The closest I've come is June, and our friendship is based solely on our positions within the church, so that isn't saying much. Still, I like June. Which is more than I can say for the rest of them.

I pick up my phone again. *Not today*, I tell myself. I won't go there today. I feel antsy, so I open Instalook again. I close it quickly; I have things to do. But not before checking the number of likes I've received on my roses. Ninety-seven so far. In thirty-eight seconds. I know it shouldn't matter— but those likes make me feel good.

I shoot a text to Grant, thanking him for the flowers. *They're beautiful,* I write. I mean it, but also, I know how much my husband appreciates reciprocation. While I wait for him to text back, my phone rings. It's June. I already know why she's calling. She's scared. I saw it this morning. She told me as much, when Grant stepped out to take a call. She thinks someone is out to get her. Grant assures me this can happen when the body is fighting an infection, when a person is really sick. But he's wrong about part of it. June was like this before he performed the breast enhancement on her. She was paranoid before the infection. He didn't say anything when I mentioned that. He doesn't like it when I worry.

"I have to pick up Avery first," I tell her.

"Can't she ride the bus?" She scoffs. "My kids always rode the bus..."

"She hates the bus, June." I don't mean to sound annoyed but maybe Grant is right. Maybe I shouldn't let her depend on me so much. It's just that she reminds me a little of Kate and Kate depended on me a lot. I guess it's good to feel needed. "No one rides the bus these days."

"Sure they do," she says. "Why else would they have them?"

I pinch the bridge of my nose and squeeze my eyes shut.

"And, you know, it might make her appreciate you a little more if she had to face a little bit of hardship. Speaking of hardship," she says lowering her voice. "I have to tell you, I think it's going to happen today. I don't care what it takes Josie—you have to do something. You have to get me out of here."

"June, please."

"Please, what?"

"We've discussed this."

She starts in on me again, and I listen for a few moments until my head throbs, and my phone buzzes.

"Avery is beeping in," I tell her. "I have to go."

"What? Who?"

"I've got to go," I repeat. "I'll be there at 5:30," I promise, and I press the button to switch calls.

"Avery—"

"Mom," I hear my daughter say on the other end of the line. She's breathless, but then that's the norm these days. Everything is urgent and everything is a disaster. This is fourteen. "I need you to pick me up," she huffs. "ASAP—we have a semester test in biology, and I have a massive headache...I can't possibly take that test today."

"Avery..."

"What? If I do, I'll seriously flunk out of school!"

"Avery, I can't pick you up right now," I sigh. "I have a long list of things to do. Can't you just stick it out?"

"Mommmmm. NO." She's annoyed with me, every bit her father's daughter. "I can't just stick it out," she swears. "Do you even realize what you're asking me?"

Of course I realize what I'm asking.

"Avery—"

"You know what?" she huffs. "Never mind. I'll just start walking home."

"Fine," I relent. I shake my head at what I'm about to say. "I'll be there in 20 minutes. Be ready and waiting on the bench."

She knows I won't let her walk home. It's an empty threat. At this age, she's still all arms and legs, outgoing and headstrong, everything that I wasn't. She's moody and impossible— all the things no one tells you about when they place that little bundle of joy in your arms.

Avery didn't speak until she was almost two and a half, and I remember practically willing her to talk. Grant swore up and down that it was that one glass of wine I had before I knew I was pregnant. *A woman should be reserved in all things.* But we both knew that wasn't it. He, more so than me, given that he's an actual doctor. I begged him to let me take her to a speech therapist, but he refused. Until one day I took her anyway. I'll never forget how I paid for that. Interestingly enough, it was a few short days after that Avery graced us with her first word. It wasn't *Mama* and it wasn't *Dada*. It was *no*.

Of course, these days things are a little different. She never shuts up, and most of the time, I remember to be thankful for that. That's not to say that I don't brace myself whenever my phone rings. I know who's calling. The church, Grant, but usually it's the kids. This is the stage of parenting where you never quite know what the call will bring. Sometimes it's a forgotten lunch, sometimes it's a needed ride, usually it's "I need money," "Can you put money in my account?" or "Can I go home with so and so after school?"

The answer is almost always yes, and I'm sure that's the problem. I once complained to Grant about it. He simply sighed, and shook his head like I was the most daft person on the planet. Afterward, he'd reminded me, this is my job, and if I only stopped to consider the stuff he has to deal with on a day-to-day basis, then maybe I wouldn't complain so much.

But he's wrong about that.

I do think about the kinds of things he has to deal with. I think about those women, how he sculpts perfect breasts. I think about their perfect bodies, the kind of precision it takes to mold the perfect face, and I can't help but wonder if he isn't right.

CHAPTER FOUR

IZZY

"Thank you for covering for me," Stacey calls out. Her voice sounds exasperated, but it's always like that. From the corner of my eye, I see her slip the apron over her head. I notice the way the corners of her lips turn up as she ties it behind her back. It makes me roll my eyes. I can't help myself. She loves this place, and I wish I had something I loved that much.

"No problem," I answer, which is pretty much the same thing as saying: *how could I say no when you offered me triple the pay?*

That's the thing about people like Stacey. She thinks I covered an extra shift to be nice, or more likely because I had nothing better to do other than save her ass. Even if she wasn't right, even if I didn't have anything on my plate not counting staring at those same beige walls and surfing the internet, that isn't the point. The point is, it never occurred to her that I might actually need the money, and why would it? Stacey came by Lucky's Sandwich Shoppe the way most people on this end of town come by the things they have. Inheritance. A member of the lucky sperm club, Stacey was born into the right family at the right time, without a care in the world, her last name practically a guarantee she'd never have to question where her next meal is going to come from. Even if she didn't own a sandwich shoppe.

This is probably why she constantly talks of closing down, although we both know she's full of it. Lucky's was her grandfather's, and she couldn't bear to see it go. It's in her blood, as she likes to say, which is another way of her saying it's a nice hobby to keep her busy, seeing that she has all the money she'll ever need. This and the fact it makes her look like she's actually contributing something to the world, even if that something is just unremarkable coffee and mediocre sandwiches in an aesthetic environment.

"No seriously," she drones on. "I really don't know what I'd do without you."

I shrug, because I'm not sure what to say to that. I don't feel that way about anyone. Maybe not even Josh, back when he was alive. Also, I'm smart enough to know it's better to say nothing when what I really want is to tell her she's being melodramatic. Thankfully, for the both of us, I know when to keep my mouth shut. About a lot of things.

Don't get me wrong, it's not that I dislike Stacey. I guess you could say I'm indifferent. We have an agreement. It's simple this way. I work. She pays. The gig feeds me, in more ways than one. It isn't all bad. There's amusement in it, at least. Stacey's one of those eternally optimistic people whose every complaint is packaged neatly, at best, and backhanded, at worst.

I finger my earrings, the ones she bought for me last month after 1 saw someone on Instalook (@luckygirl242) wearing a pair and commented how much I liked them. She likes to do that, surprise me with things, just because she can. It'd be nice to say I appreciate her gestures. But mostly, it makes me hate her a little bit.

~

I TYPE MY EMPLOYEE NUMBER INTO THE COMPUTER (3-2-1),

officially clocking myself out. Finally. I've been counting the minutes to freedom. I'm in a hurry, so I wipe my hands on my jeans and instantly I regret it. They're my favorite pair. I splurged on them after @fashionistaforver777 posted pictures on Instalook calling them *on trend*. Thinking of her now, I close my eyes and exhale. I shake my head. *If you hadn't gotten so close, you wouldn't have been so let down.* @Fashionistaforver777 also known as Alice IRL (in real life) used to be one of my favorites to follow. I loved her vacation photos, and her makeup tricks, despite the fact that I couldn't afford any of them. Well, not really.

It was her husband Saul who really drew me in. He loved her. I could always tell when it was him behind the lens. And so, when she announced her divorce, that was it for me— I couldn't go on pretending to want to dress and look and vacation like her, when she was clearly not appreciative of any of it. She tossed Saul aside like she tossed the latest (#solastseason) trend. I shouldn't have let it get me down the way it did. Things meant nothing to her. So why would people?

"See you in a few," Stacey calls through the door, bringing me back to the here and now. It's not a question, and I'm not sure how much of that is part of the problem for me. Before today, before I saw the two of them, I considered packing it all up. I thought about disappearing, getting away from this place. I thought what I needed was a fresh start. But seeing Grant Dunn and his lovely wife gave me hope, and now I'm not so sure. Maybe this morning won't be my last shift after all.

"See you for second shift," I say on my way out, unusually upbeat, and I actually mean it. For the first time in a long time, I'm buzzing with excitement. I don't even make it to the car before I'm tapping the letters into my screen. I check Instalook for his name first. No dice. Then I go straight to Google. *Grant Dunn.* Tell me. Who are you? Who is that you're married to? And, where do the two of you like to play online?

CHAPTER FIVE

JOSIE

"You're home early."

"Sit down, Jos—" Grant tells me, kissing my cheek.

I'm washing something in the sink, and I have to turn so I can see his face. Something is off. It's there in the crease between his brow.

"What?" I ask, cocking my head. I turn off the faucet and dry my hands. "What is it?"

He presses his lips together and takes a deep breath in. "June is dead."

The news comes out on the exhale, like it was nothing at all. I drop the towel I'm holding. Just let go. I shake my head. This can't be right. "I just saw her."

He smacks his lips and readies his doctor voice. The one with authority. "She died at 14:00."

I suck my bottom lip between my teeth and hold it there. I can't compute what he's saying. Also, this is not an occasion that calls for military time. It takes me a few seconds to mentally calculate what that means. Finally, it hits me. "I don't understand."

"The infection was worse than they thought," he says, scanning

BRITNEY KING

the mail I left for him on the counter. When I don't say anything, he looks up. "She turned septic."

I can't breathe. My lungs are seizing. "How can that be? I just talked to her...a few hours ago."

"I'm sorry Josie," he says, setting the mail aside. He walks over to where I'm standing. "That's just how it works out sometimes."

I collapse into his arms, and I want to cry, I really do. For June. For the guilt I feel. Instead I feel numb. He holds me for several long moments, and then he pulls back and looks into my eyes. "I brought you something from the hospital."

He leaves me to walk over to his bag. I stare at the towel on the floor. I mean to pick it up, but I can't make myself. Grant does it. He hates anything out of place. "Here," he says. My vision is blurry. *I shouldn't have been so short with her.*

"Josie," he says. "I brought this for you." I think he's going to hand me something of June's, but he doesn't. Instead, he places a well-worn book in my hands. *How To Cope With Sudden Loss.* I turn it over, and Grant turns to go. I thank him, and then I remove my phone from my pocket and snap a photo of the book in one hand. I make sure my new heels are in the shot, too, because I've been meaning to post about them. I caption the shot: Hug your loved ones close. You never know. #nothingrealeverdies

It's a silly thing to do, but all over town, other members of New Hope are getting the news too. I have to be a leader. I have to stay on top of things. June would understand.

Grant interrupts me by asking where the kids are. I point upstairs, press the button to upload the photo, and that is that.

THREE WEEKS LATER IT FEELS LIKE DÉJÀ VU WHEN GRANT COMES walking in the door before dark.

I look up from my phone. "You're home early."

"We have a dinner," he tells me, kissing my cheek.

44

I cock my head. "But I made dinner." This is random, out of the blue. My husband hates anything out of the blue. In his line of work, the unexpected never signifies anything good.

I await his response, but none comes. His face is relaxed. He smiles. He takes me in his arms. "I can't wait to show you off."

I grin. His mood feels contagious. Trouble is, I just fixed the most amazing meal, and I've already uploaded the spread in my dining room to Instalook, and I'm not sure how I'll fit this into my feed. Then a hashtag comes to mind— #husbandhadotherplans then #blesssedlife and instantly I feel better, knowing there's a solution. "Why didn't you tell me before?"

He pulls away. "Tom is back," he tells me nonchalantly.

I bite my lip. "Tom?"

His whole demeanor changes. He leans down, and then hands me his things to put away. He could do it himself, but he's used to having nurses and assistants take care of the minutiae for him. Why should it be any different at home? *Habits are hard to break.* He always says that.

"Did he bring her?" I tread carefully.

I watch my husband's expression, blank as he mulls over what I've asked. "Of course he brought her."

I scan the room, looking for a way out. "In that case—I don't know if I can go…"

He cocks his head, shuffles his feet, and then crosses one ankle over the other. It's as though he hasn't heard me. Until he meets my eye. "You can go."

My stomach flip-flops. It doesn't help that it's empty. "It just feels like such a betrayal to June. I just don't get it—it hasn't even been that long."

The corners of his eyes crinkle. I can see that he's analyzing me carefully. "June is dead."

"Yes. But I don't know…" I admit as I dry my hands. *Idle hands are the devil's workshop.* "I think something is off." I turn toward him. "It doesn't seem right that he'd do this, Grant. Also—she said things—she said someone was out to get her."

He shrugs.

"That doesn't seem like the June I knew…"

He walks over to where I'm standing and runs his hands down the lengths of my arms. I close my eyes. Bile rises. Grant hates being challenged. Everything in me tenses. He sighs deeply before he leans forward and kisses my forehead. "June was sick, dear. Shame makes people do all sorts of things."

"Shame?"

He glances up at the ceiling, and then back at me. "Ok, grief."

I don't say anything. I miss June. I feel terrible about what happened. But if I feel grief over the loss, it has to do with more than the fact that she's not around anymore. He steps away. I watch as he retrieves his phone from his pocket. I take note of the time on the clock above the oven as he stares intently at the screen. When just enough time has passed that it doesn't seem confrontational, I say, "I just don't see how he could replace her so soon."

He raises his head slowly. I think I see disappointment in his eyes. "What choice did he have?"

I purse my lips and busy myself with cleaning up the meal that will go to waste. I don't know what he means by choice, but I know better than to ask. Sometimes it's best to avoid the hard stuff. Grant abhors all forms of gossip. It's firmly and righteously against our agreement.

He exhales loudly.

"Long day?" I ask because it's too early in the evening for him to be this irritated on account of me. Not if tonight is going to turn out well.

"They added another surgery onto my schedule tomorrow."

I pick up a knife and scrape my effort into the trash bin.

Grant clears his throat. "You will be kind to her, Jos—we can't afford anymore mishaps. Not if we want to remain a part of the congregation."

Truth be told, I don't really know whether or not I want to remain a member of New Hope. It has its benefits sure. But it has major drawbacks, too. My husband likes to allude to the fact that they'll kick us out. "They won't kick you out—they need you too much."

"Who knows what they'll do, Josie."

"I'll get dressed," I say, changing the subject. Mishaps are not something either of us are in the mood to discuss.

"Where are the kids?" he asks as I straighten the mail he's just tossed on the table.

"Avery is at Carly's. She's staying the night. And James is upstairs working on homework."

My husband does a double-take. "You let her go to the Clarks?"

I furrow my brow. "You told her she could, remember?" It's not the whole truth, of course. She asked him when he was distracted, and he answered in kind.

"The Clarks are under investigation," he says matter-of-factly.

"What?" I drop the mail. "You didn't tell me—"

He scoffs. "You know the rules."

Boy, do I ever.

I wait for him to say more, but he closes his eyes instead. I hold my breath. It's always been my mission to keep the kids out of these things. "I can't tell you every detail of everything, Josie. Sometimes you have to think for yourself."

"But this applies to our child, Grant. You could've said something."

"I didn't tell her she could go," he assures me. "I would remember that."

"Should I call her home?"

He considers my question, although I know my husband. He's already thought it through. "No," he says finally. "It's a minor infraction," he adds. He chooses his words carefully. "Something in an audit. A red flag...I don't think we should make a big deal out of it. Yet."

Yet. A minor infraction could mean a lot of things. But so far as I know, the Clarks have always had a good track record. I exhale deeply. I'm lightheaded either from holding my breath or not eating.

I need to know how bad it might be. "What did they do?"

"You know I can't tell you that Jos—why do you even ask?"

"Because Avery and her safety mean more to me than anything in this world," I say, and immediately I know it was both the wrong and the right thing to say.

"I see," he says. "It's nice to know where I rank in your little world."

I lean against the counter, and he does the same. We stand facing each other. He places his phone in his pocket, and then watches me for several moments. "It's nothing you should worry about, love."

But I do worry. My husband is third in command at New Hope. It can be dangerous for him, and thus for those related to him, if another member is backed into a corner. This alone is why he should tell me.

"You know talking about the infractions of others is prohibited."

"But I'm your wife. And this is our child we're talking about."

"What are you suggesting? That I'm being reckless, insensitive —or both?"

"Neither. I just want reassurance is all."

"Nothing is guaranteed in life, Josie. You of all people should know that."

I don't know what he means.

He crosses and uncrosses his arms. "You know, Dan was telling me we ought to replace the tile in the clubhouse. And I was thinking he might be right," he says widening his stance.

"Although— the more I think of it, the more I realize with the right amount of effort we could really get it shining again. Put the money saved toward recruitment efforts." He studies my face. "Don't you think?"

I don't answer. I know where this is headed. What I don't know is why he's changing the subject.

"I'll leave the supplies for you here in the morning." He points to the counter. "Should give you plenty of time to think about where we stand."

"Grant," I plead. "I have a full day tomorrow."

"Yes," he says. "I'm sure you do. But we really need to get that floor in shape."

"Maybe Dan is right," I suggest. "Maybe we should just replace it."

His eyes shift, but just a little before his expression becomes fixed once again. "Sometimes taking the easy way out isn't always the best way, love." He smiles. "Just ask June."

CHAPTER SIX

IZZY

The aroma hits me immediately as I place my key in the lock. I fling the door open faster than I intend to. The wave of garbage hits me. *Shit.* I don't have the time or the patience for this. Not now. All I want to do is sink down onto the couch and scan through Instalook. We were so busy today that I didn't get much of a chance, and my mind is reeling with all that I missed. Now Instalook is going to have to wait because there's no mistaking the smell that fills my tiny apartment. It only takes two tiny breaths for me to realize its origin and my mistake. I accidentally left last night's take out in the trash.

Take out I barely touched, which explains the overwhelming stench.

I curse myself. Not only am I missing out on what's happening on Instalook, but also, I have research to do. I can't believe how stupid I am— I shouldn't be so forgetful. It's just that it was always his job, the trash, which is clearly why my apartment reeks of warm, putrid, rotting food. I begin to dry-heave. Sweat beads at my temples. I can't afford to set the AC lower than eighty-two, which doesn't help with the smell. I could faint at any moment. Who knows how long it would be before anyone found me?

The wretched smell wafting from my apartment should be a dead giveaway, but apparently, no one in this building cares. These days, people are willing to look the other way. Everyone has their own problems. I once saw a story on the internet where an elderly woman was dead in her house for eight months before anyone thought to look for her. That would be me. Only younger.

I massage my temples and turn the air conditioner all the way down. Fuck it, who cares about paying your electricity bill if you won't survive to see it come? I toss my keys onto the counter, and I can almost hear his voice in my mind. *Lock the door, Izzy. Lock the door.* But I don't lock the door. It feels kind of nice to be brazen, now that he's not here to stop me. It feels like playing Russian roulette with my life, and before today, before I saw them, taking chances like this was the only thing that brought me even an ounce of satisfaction. Locking the door doesn't matter much anymore.

Not even on this side of town.

When it's your time to go, it's your time to go. *Damn it, Izzy,* I hear him say. *Why can't you ever listen?* I cover my ears. I hate it. I hate his voice. I hate that he's still bouncing around in my head, and yet at the same time, I don't want to consider the alternative. There's no telling how long I'll keep hearing him speak to me. *How long will I remember what he sounds like? How long will I know what he would have said? A year? Five years? Forever?*

I suck a deep breath in, pinch my nose with one hand, and with the other I take the trash sack from the garbage, and set it out in the hall. On my way back in, I spot the mail I left on the counter yesterday. As I scan through the envelopes, I can see that it's all the same: bills, bills, and more bills. It never ends. At least there were no boxes today. Three days running, and the delivery-man has stayed away. This is a record for me. Of course, it isn't just sheer willpower—I only have one credit card that isn't maxed, and mama taught me at least one thing: drown if you must, but know how to save yourself if you change your mind. Suddenly, I feel that familiar softness circling my ankles. I kick Whiskers away. I hate that cat. He butts his head against my lower legs, and I part them. It's like he knows.

I scoot away. He follows.

Eventually, I give up. I pick up a bill and the lighter that sits on the counter, and I hold the edge of the envelope to the flame. Fire smells better than rotting food. And it gets rid of the evidence. Usually. I watch those shows. Investigators are smart these days. You have to be smarter. You have to be like Whiskers. Relentless. He goes around my legs and through, in and out, in and out. I know what he wants, besides playing ring around the rosy with my legs. I know I forgot to feed him this morning, and yet it seems like too much work just to open a can of food. That's something else Josh always took care of. It was his cat, after all.

"No," I tell him, and my voice reverberates off the walls. *No. That's what I should have said. Don't go. I don't really need that after all.* A thousand times, I should have said it. Now, my silence is the loudest sound in the room. Hell, now it's the *only* sound in the room. I decide the cat can wait—at least until I've checked social media. At least until I've seen their faces. I toss the burning envelope in the sink. Smoke has filled the kitchen. I watch it burn for a moment, and then I turn on the water.

Whiskers meows. "Fuck you," I cough. "You're just another somebody demanding service," I say, tugging at his ear. It's not like I was the one who wanted the cat in the first place. I said no pets. I have bad luck with pets. But when Whiskers showed up, just a tiny orange kitten, starving to death and crying on our doorstep, it was Josh who caved and brought him inside. *Feed them once, my mother used to say, and they'll never go away.* I told him that too—not that he listened. He said he couldn't possibly leave him there to starve. After all, he had to live with himself. It's too bad he didn't feel the same way about leaving me.

I nudge Whiskers away with my foot. "Go."

My voice filling the empty space sends chills down my spine.

I feel the blood come rushing to my ears; I feel my heart begin to race, and I know what comes next. I sink to the floor, curl into a ball, and cover my ears. I think about all of my friends on Instalook. They're calling out to me. I flip through their profiles, in my mind, one by one, until eventually I can see straight again. I think about all the things I have to buy, all the things they want me to know about, all the ways we can be alike, until eventually, I decide three days is good.

It's been a good streak.

But my mama was wrong about a lot of things, so she was probably wrong about that too. Nothing good comes from being conservative. Moderation is for boring people. And I refuse to be that. Josh said I was destined, that we were destined for a big life, and I can't let him down. Not now. Not since he died for our cause.

I hop online, and I buy that scarf I saw the other day on @livingwithlulu547. It was featured on her "fifty faves under fifty dollars" post, so it's practically a steal. Once that's done, I picture myself wearing it, and suddenly I am not thinking about dead husbands or empty apartments or bankruptcy. I'm thinking about abundance. @livingwithlulu547 knows a thing or two about that too. She's always posting quotes, and it's like I could be living with her. If my feelings were as superficial as her makeup hacks, that is.

I need more than good lighting and finding the perfect angle.

I need something deep.

That's why I'm thinking about that beautiful couple, about how much he must love her. I'm thinking about Americanos and summer dresses and what kind of perfume she was wearing. I'm thinking that if I'm extra nice, maybe Stacey will offer to buy me that kind too. Then I can save room on my credit card for the other things I'll need to win them over. Anyway, I met @livingwithlulu547 and she wasn't all that. Not in real life. Get this, her name isn't even Lulu. It's Sharon.

Don't get me wrong, I like her style. But it could never be

more than that. This is how I know that if I can just see that couple again, it'll help. I'll feel better about the last one, who didn't work out. I'll feel grounded. Maybe I'll even be able to force down a little food.

Although, it's not food that I need. I followed a man on Instalook who has gone two years without eating a single thing. He travels the world and survives on coconut water. I didn't even know they had coconuts in all the places he visits. I wrote him about it, and he says he has them shipped in. This gave me hope. There really are people out there willing to go the extra mile. People like Josh. That's what I need, more than food. I need hope.

I plop down on the couch and open my laptop, click on the browser and type in his name. Grant Dunn. I haven't seen anything concrete in regard to the places they frequent, which is why I haven't quite figured out our next meet-up.

But I tell myself not to give up.

I will see them in person again. Once can't have been it for us. I breathe easier as their photos load on the screen. I have loved getting to know them, learning their likes and their dislikes. I may not yet know where she hangs out in real life, but I know everything else. I know what Josie Dunn reads, I know her favorite flower—antique roses. I know she hates cats, and that laundry is her nemesis, and that she's allergic to shellfish. *One can never be too careful.* I know I won't have a 'chance encounter' with her in a seafood restaurant. Still, it makes me so happy to see their faces. I keep looking. I keep checking Instalook for a sign. *Tell me where to go.* It only takes one post about the future, one shred of something concrete. I know if I'm diligent—if I'm careful enough— I'll find what I'm looking for. Even though I knew the moment they walked into my shop, I already had.

CHAPTER SEVEN

JOSIE

I listen as Grant checks in on James. I can't hear most of their exchange, but I overhear the last of it. We're set to leave in an hour. I check the time, and then I go into the walk in closet and try to gauge what my husband might like me to wear. Eventually, he comes back into the room—I can tell by the way the hairs on the back of my neck stand on end. They've done that since the first time I laid eyes on him. Of course, now it means something very different than it did back then.

"Well," he says, his voice deep and smooth. In control. "Let's see what you chose."

I hold up the little black dress. These days I like safe bets.

"Hmmm," he says, eyeing me up and down.

"What?" I ask, because I know it's what he wants. Sometimes my husband wants to spell it out, and sometimes he likes to play.

He rubs his jaw and then pauses mid-rub. "I don't think we're on the same wavelength tonight, you and I..."

I lean back against the wall and study my husband. I feel that familiar pang in the pit of my stomach. *Longing.* Longing for what, I'm not sure. It's complicated. Like my wardrobe selection. He wants to play. Fine. I place my hands on my hips and offer a sly smile. "What would you have me wear?"

"One of the upsides of being married to one of the top plastic surgeons in the country is having a large wardrobe, Mrs. Dunn. And this—" he says holding up the dress "is what you choose? "

I take it from his hands. "Yes, because the downside is—you are constantly on display."

I feel the back of his hand reverberate off my left cheek. I feel the sting, the weight of his hand as the blood pools to the surface. But I didn't see it coming. Mostly, I don't. Instinctively, my hand goes to my face. I feel the burn, and I cower.

When I'm able to look up, I see my husband wringing his hand. *He thinks it hurts.*

"I told you not to test me, Josie. You know how I feel about disrespect." He swings his hands wildly, motioning around the large walk-in closet. It's big, big enough to be a spare bedroom. Sometimes it is. "I give you all of this and for what? To have my life—our life—mocked?"

"I'm not mocking you," I cry. I don't mean to. Rarely can I help it.

"You're telling me you didn't know going in that there would be…certain expectations?"

"No, I knew."

"So then what? It's not okay to want my wife to look good when I take her out?"

"No," I say staring at the floor. "I didn't mean—."

He takes my chin and lifts it so my eyes align with his. My teeth dig into my tongue. *He won't want to cancel. Which means he won't leave a mark.*

"Then what did you mean?"

I shake my head. Not much because it's in his hands. "I don't know."

"I think you do know. Don't take me for a fool, Josie. And I won't take you for one. Lest you forget what's at stake here. If you can't be what I want you to be then just say the words—if this is not what you want— you know where the door is. You've always known."

He's right; I do know what's at stake. Everything. My husband isn't a fool. We both know that.

"Is this what you want? Us? This family?"

"Of course."

"Because, you know how easy it would be to let it all go, don't you? I've always told you...I'll set you up in a little apartment— you know the kind—and we'll call it a day."

"And the kids? What about the kids?" He likes it when I bring this up. It hammers me into place.

"They'll stay here, of course. Where they're comfortable."

I know what he means. He doesn't have to say it. He controls everything. The money he off-shores, or ties up in his business— and the house is in the church's name—so, in the end, he's right. I'll come out with very little.

"Anyway. Let me remind you. You like appearances, no?" He glances at my phone. "What kind of job do you think you'll get? Money guarantees beauty. My profession is a testament to that. But it doesn't always work the other way around, now does it? You'll need a skill set to land you a job." He scoffs. I look at the floor. "What do you think that might be? At your age? Lunching? Carpool? Gardening? Reading? I'm glad you have your hobbies. Don't get me wrong; that's why I work so hard. But let's face it, what you have are hardly employable skills, darling."

He shifts my chin forcing me to look at him. I've heard this all before. "It was just an off the cuff remark," I say. "I didn't mean anything by it."

He touches my face. "And I didn't mean to put my hands on you."

I nod like I understand, and I do. I understand that he chooses his words carefully. He doesn't say, *I didn't mean to hit you. Slapping you was an accident, I meant nothing by it.* No, not my husband. He's precise. Careful.

This makes me realize I should be too.

I RUN MY FINGERS OVER THE DRESSES. I COLLECT MYSELF, GET MY emotions in check. I select a green silk A-line dress Grant bought for me during his last trip to Argentina. I'm guessing he'll like this one. It holds memories.

I snap a photo of it next to a sheer blue wraparound and post it to Instalook with the caption: Decisions. Decisions. What say you?

Almost instantly, I have ninety-two responses, and I realize I was right to go with the A-line.

"I'd like to lie with you before we go," Grant calls out from the bedroom. It catches me off-guard given our argument. That's not to say I'm surprised. I know him.

"Just a sec—" I hold the dress up to my frame and wonder if I hurry to throw it on whether it'd make any difference. Probably not. I'd just have to find something else to wear. He steps into the closet. When I don't answer, because there isn't one, he repeats himself. "I said I want to lie with you before we go."

I know what this means, and I meet his eye accordingly.

"I have to get ready," I say, glancing at the clock.

"Being late is fashionable, Mrs. Dunn." He's standing just behind me, running his hands over my hips. He's lying. He doesn't like to be late.

I watch his hands in the mirror. They're cold. "What do you think about this dress?" I ask, a considerate distraction.

"I think— I like what is underneath the dress better."

His response tells me what I need to know. I won't be getting out of it tonight. Not that I've ever really been that successful. We have an agreement. It's one every couple at New Hope shares: one is never to refuse their spouse. It's written in the Bible.

"Josie," he repeats, his tone stern. "I said, I want to lie with you."

This time I do as he asks, without hesitation. I hang the dress over the door, and I turn to him.

He waits for me to exit the closet, and his eyes never leave mine as I walk across the room. I get into bed and eventually he climbs in on top of me. I swallow hard at the weight of his body on mine. He smooths my hair away from my face. "Do you love me?"

"Of course," I tell him.

He stares into my eyes, and it's like he can see right through me, to the depths of my soul. "I am so lucky," he says, after a long, slow exhale. "To be going to dinner with you. To be married to you. To have you in my bed. This is what it's all about, Josie. The sacrifice. This," he says motioning to the small, ever-shrinking space between us. "This is what it's all about."

I nod and offer the most sincere smile I can muster.

He kisses the spot just between my eyes, and he's so gentle. It kills me. "You will be the most beautiful woman there. Without a doubt. It pains me," he says, wincing. "I will have to share you with everyone, which you know I hate doing. But when I look across the room and your eyes meet mine, I will know."

I can see he wants me to ask. So I do. "You'll know what?"

His lips trail lower and lower. I grip the sheets. "I will know the flush on your cheeks is because of me," he says, and he pauses long enough to look up and smile from down below. "And that, my love, will be a gift to us both."

I want to be angry, lying there, with his head between my legs. I want to hate him for asking me to do this here, now, after what just happened in the closet. But he doesn't make it easy. "You are so beautiful when you give in," he tells me as he moves inside of me.

A moan escapes my lips because he knows all the right places to touch, all the right things to say. He knows what to do to get the reaction he wants. That's what he does. He sculpts things—people, faces, breasts, asses—he sculpts them to perfection. He's perfected everything, even our lovemaking, down to an art, down to an exact science. That's how he works. He's learned how to get my body to respond every time, and without fail, it does. "Just let go, Jos—" he urges. He pushes on the edges of my instability. "You just have to let go."

And so I do. I lie there, and I picture myself as a balloon tethered to something intangible. I watch myself come undone until I am floating free. Up, up, and away.

CHAPTER EIGHT

IZZY

I check Instalook for the hundredth time and this time there's a new post from one-half of my favorite couple. Finally. It's a picture of two dresses, and she wants me to choose. I like that she makes things interactive. I choose the green one but not just because it'll look great on her. Smart people always choose green; I read that once. Plus, it would look amazing on me. I can see myself in that dress. I can feel the fabric on my skin. I close my eyes and imagine the way Grant Dunn will look at her from across the room in that dress. I imagine the way he would look at me. The way everyone would.

I stay there for a moment, letting my mind run wild. I follow Kelsey @liveyourbestlife224 on Instalook, and she says visualization is a key factor in getting what you want. I believe her; she should know—she's practically posting in a different yoga pose on a different mountain top every other day. Not only is she flexible and fit, she makes them both look better by being high above the rest of us. Anyway, she seems good at getting what she wants. She doesn't burn her fingertips raw making other people's dreams come true. She doesn't wipe countertops all day long and still break a sweat when the bills come due. Not her. She's living her best life and mine too.

I start to feel the rage build, and I know it's time to take a break. It takes a lot out of a person to imagine all the things they don't have. I get up and go into the kitchen. Whiskers takes it as an invitation. He meows, rubs up on my legs and follows me around the tiny space. I don't feed him. If I can't have what I want, then neither can he. Cats don't need to eat everyday, anyway. They're natural hunters. I check the fridge. It's pretty much empty, save for a carton of expired milk and a box of takeout that's so old I can't recall how long it's been in there. I should just throw it away. But it seems like a lot of effort. And I have to save my energy. Focus on the things that matter. That's what you do when you're living your best life. I grab a can of Diet Coke. It's all there is. I don't even like Diet Coke. It was Josh's, but he's dead so he won't mind.

I pop the tab, and Whiskers comes running. He jumps up on the couch next to me, and I shoo him away. He remembers that sound. "Fuck you, and your cat too," I say into thin air. I don't know if the dead can hear, but I hope so.

I need something to take my mind off of dead husbands, annoying cats, and empty apartments. I open Instalook again and read Josie's comments. Most people chose the green dress. But that's not what I'm looking for. I don't care what they choose. I'm looking for something else. I see her and her enthusiastic responses. I see that she's happy, abundant, living her best life. What I don't see is where I might find her: where she's wearing that perfect dress, with that perfect husband. This is irritating. I'm on edge. Now that I know more, but not what I want, I know too much. The dress she posted about is not only gorgeous and not at all my size, but also it came from Argentina, and the odds of me going there are pretty much slim to none.

It's impulsive, but it comes to me. This grand idea. Within

three seconds flat, I'm staring at photos of people cramming sea creatures down their throats. You can find pretty much anything on the internet. If you can imagine it, I bet you can find it. I know because there are hundreds, if not thousands, of people eating shellfish filling my screen. My head pounds, and nothing is clear. Well, one thing is clear: I have to do this. I should have been a little more brazen the last time, and I wouldn't have lost. This time, I know better. And as @livingyourbestlife224 says: when you know better, you do better. Okay, maybe that was Maya Angelou. But still. I have to feel something. I spent all day waiting on people, whipping up their every whim (you wouldn't believe the bullshit requests people come up with) and doing it with a smile. And what do I have to show for it? A meager, unlivable wage, and a guarantee that I get to do it all again tomorrow. I download the photos, ninety-eight of them to be exact, and then I consider my next move. I don't have to send them. Sometimes it's nice to know there's a weapon to draw should you need it. What I need now is food. Creativity takes a lot out of a person. I set my laptop aside and go to the kitchen. This time I retrieve a can of tuna from the cabinet. I'm not supposed to eat it; it's a part of Josh's survival kit, reserved for the end of the world times, but what can I say? All of those happy people eating their seafood got to me.

Of course, Whiskers is all over it. Finally, just so I can eat my tuna and crackers in peace, I open the fridge and pour the expired milk into a bowl. "There," I say, patting his head. I don't think he'll drink it. But he does.

After the tuna, I remember the bottle of champagne under the sink. Stacey gave it to me a few months ago when she went on one of those whole foods diets. Needless to say, she's still overweight, and I still have the bottle. I don't know why but this feels like something worth celebrating. If Grant and Josie Dunn get to have a good time, then so do I.

When I wake up in the morning, the bottle is empty, the cat has shit all over the apartment, and I've sent all ninety-eight very strange pictures of highly allergic people eating shellfish to Josie Dunn, posing as one of her followers, and the latter is the only reason I want to get off the couch. I have to make things right again.

CHAPTER NINE

JOSIE

The first thing I notice is how young she looks. Of course, she does. My breath catches as Tom scoots from behind the door cautiously, and that's when I see Winnie, her tail wagging. She's ready to pounce. She'll ruin the dress, I realize this, but in that moment, I'm just so surprised that I don't immediately make a move to block her. Tom grabs the dog by the collar as his new bride looks on, adoration plastered across her face. I should be watching Winnie, but I'm not. She's perfect, this girl. Perfect for Tom. Perfect all-around. "Grant...Josie," Tom says, looking up, also panting, his face in full grin. "This is Mel."

She extends her hand to me, and I take it in mine. "Welcome to the neighborhood."

Her face lights up and her chest deflates. I can feel her relief through her fingertips. "It's every bit as lovely as Tom told me it would be."

"It's a pleasure," Grant offers, bringing her hand to his lips. "I've heard so much about you."

She giggles. She actually fucking giggles. Like a schoolgirl. I shouldn't be surprised; it isn't so much a stretch.

"Come in," Tom motions, ushering us through the foyer. "Make yourself at home."

And I do feel at home. Nothing has changed from the time June lived here, just weeks ago. I don't know what I expected, but it wasn't that everything would be the same.

"Josie." I hear my name. I'd recognize that shrill voice anywhere. I turn to see Beth standing there, her hands on her hips. She's displeased with me, as usual. "Thank God," she says, taking the bottle of wine I'm holding. "You're late. And we're already out of white."

Beth is my 'sponsor,' and has been from the time her husband initiated New Hope.

I smile and lean in to kiss both her cheeks. "It's good to see you, too."

She takes my hands and gives them a squeeze. "When are you ever going to learn to be on time?" she chides as she kisses each of my cheeks. It would be nice to say we're on equal footing, Beth and I. But seeing that her husband is the founder of New Hope, that isn't the case. In reality, we actually don't care much for one another. But you wouldn't know it by the amount of time we spend together. Mondays it's coffee at my house at 8:00 a.m. sharp. Thursdays it's tea at hers. Fridays we hold committee for the other wives, and sometimes we do brunch on Saturdays while our husbands golf. At New Hope, we treat religion like a twelve-step program. It works better this way.

"Everything is so organized," Mel says, meeting my eye. "I just hope I've done my part."

"You've done your part," I tell her, thinking of June. I know I shouldn't place the blame on her—she is so young, after all, but I can't help myself. June was my friend, like Kate was my friend, only different. I offer a reassuring smile just for Beth. "You weren't supposed to do anything, really," I say, and it isn't a lie. This time it's my turn. "That's why we're here—to honor you."

Beth raises her brow. "Josie is right. We want you to feel welcome."

"Everything is so...well thought out," Mel tells her.

Beth laughs and fans her dress. "We pride ourselves on excellence at New Hope." A server stops by with a tray of appetizers. I watch as she carefully selects the one she wants. When she's satisfied, she turns back to us. "Well, that's the mission, anyway."

"I'm very impressed. Tom speaks highly of the church—about how it changed his life."

"Ah," Beth says. She speaks firmly, authoritatively, as though she's trying to establish her rightful place in the girl's mind. Also, she never misses a chance to talk up the church. "Tom was perfect for New Hope from the get go. He's very meticulous in that way."

"That he is." Mel lights up. "Sometimes I wonder how I'll ever keep up."

"You will," Beth assures her. "You have us. We stick together at New Hope," she says with a smile. "Also, this is why I wanted to introduce you to Josie. She is to be your sponsor."

I do a double-take. This is the first I've heard of this.

Beth's eyes widen. She looks thrilled. I can see she's pleased with herself for breaking the news. "I think the two of you will get on quite well."

Mel smiles in her naïve, girlish way. "I'm excited to learn the ropes."

"You'll catch on," I say pursing my lips. "Although I think Beth would be the better woman to teach you."

"Nonsense," Beth laughs. "Who do you think taught you?"

"You have a point," I agree. It's easier this way. Beth did teach me everything I know. Even now, she's teaching me.

"I'm just excited to really dive in. From what Tom has told me, it seems like you guys have created the perfect church home. And you know... it's funny. This was something I've been searching for, for so, so long. I can't even begin to tell you. And so...to know it was here—that it was out there all along—well—I just feel so blessed, you know?"

Beth's palm flies to her chest. She's touched. New Hope is her baby and every bit as important to her as her real children. This church and the way it works is her brain-child. It's her whole life, a point she likes to drive home often. I watch carefully as she takes a quick breath in and lets it out. "We started the congregation hoping there were people out there like you," she says, leaning forward. "But you never really know, you know? Some things just hit, while others don't. Thankfully, we've been very fortunate with New Hope in that regard."

I listen as she speaks, wondering how much I can still force myself to believe. Once upon a time I was as green as Mel. These days I wish I was that young, that innocent, that full of goodwill.

"GOODWILL," BETH SAYS, ADDRESSING THE GROUP AND SUDDENLY I'm transported back to her living room, back to the beginning. She smiles proudly. "That's what we need," she adds, and back then she was as much of a liar as she is now. Back then, we didn't need fancy buildings or recruitment strategies or weekly weigh-ins. Back then, we just needed each other. Or so I thought. Or so we all thought.

I can still picture her there in her tweed skirt and sweater, looking girlish and alive. We were all tired, in the early days of parenting and trying to build careers, this in addition to managing things at home while our husbands worked long, relentless hours. Beth was one of those women we all looked up to. Even if we didn't exactly like her, we admired her, nonetheless. She didn't look haggard or withdrawn like the rest of us. She was making a list and taking names, in heels and makeup, no less. With two well-behaved children hanging off each leg.

She extends her arms as though she's been practicing for this speech her whole life. "We need to bring goodwill back into our lives. We need to bring excellence back to the table. We need to instill this in our children. We need to model it in our marriages."

The seven of us nodded in unison. Her speech was moving. We were inspired. We all wanted a change. We all wanted to not feel so alone. Hell, what we all wanted more than anything was adult conversation, and for that reason alone, no matter what Beth had said, we would have agreed.

Then, while New Hope was in its infancy, a string of terrible events happened in our city, in our neighborhood, right under our noses, and what we all wanted more than anything was to know how we'd failed to see that women were being trafficked right under our noses. We missed that evil lived among us, disguised as friends and neighbors. We all wanted to know what we could do to avoid it happening again. To band together, as Beth suggested, seemed like as viable an answer as any. We had to get stronger, more exclusive; we had to protect ourselves, our children, our community. It was a game-changer for most of us. But it wasn't what it is now. Back then, we were all scared—a different kind of scared than we are now. In those days, we were young and naive and full of hope. Full of belief that with each other and a few shifts we could change our lives. We managed that all right, and it changed everything.

"This is an agreement," Beth said, passing out binders. "I want you to read over it and then we will all sign it."

"And if we don't?" I asked. "If we don't sign?"

Beth glared at me, a stone-cold look in her eye. She was still angry with me about Kate and the other thing.

"Well," she laughed. "That's a great question, Josie. I'm so glad you asked. If you don't sign, then it just goes to show you don't believe in New Hope or our mission."

I nodded, and I didn't respond. I wanted to believe.

❧

"Josie," Beth calls again. "Hellllloooo." She cranes her neck. "Where are you?"

"Sorry," I shrug, her surgically enhanced nose coming into focus. "I hardly slept last night." I realize immediately this was the wrong thing to say. It's an offhand remark, an easy excuse for drifting off, for not listening to the conversation. But the little things are the things one has to be careful of. Sleep is written into the agreement. It's not wise to openly admit you're not in accordance with the agreement.

"Darling, that dress—" She leans forward to take me in, expertly changing the subject. I would like to think my comment has flown over her head—that it was lost in the moment—but I know Beth, and I know that is not the case. "It's stunning."

"Yes," Mel says. "It's perfection."

I glance down, smooth it out, and I smile. I search the crowd that's gathered in the dining area. I'm looking for my husband. It takes me a few seconds, but I spot him standing by the bar. I can't see who he's talking to, I can only just make out the back of his head. I'd know it anywhere. Another server walks by, this time with a tray of wine, and I take a glass. "Thank you," I say, meeting Mel's eye. I motion toward the dress. "Grant brought it back from Argentina."

I study her expression; she's young, but I can see that she's smart. "Where are you from?"

"Boise."

I tilt my head, jut out my lip and feign surprise. "Boise."

"Yes," she laughs. "That's where I met Tom, actually. He was there on business and walked right into me on the street." She extends her brow. "What are the odds of that?"

Pretty good, knowing Tom, I want to say. I bite my tongue.

"Anyway," she adds. "He invited me to coffee, and the rest, well, the rest is history."

"I bet it is." I don't mean to say it, I am so busy holding other things in that the words just roll on out.

"Josie!" Beth chides

"What?" I ask, brushing her off. I glance around the room, and then take a giant gulp of my wine. I look over at Beth, and I half-laugh, setting up what I'm about to say. "Everyone appreciates a good love story. I was just saying I want more— that's all."

"As her sponsor, I'm sure you'll get it," Beth assures me. *Patience is a virtue.*

"What exactly does a sponsor do?" Mel asks, scanning the crowd. I think she too is trying to cut and run, anxious to get out from underneath Beth's intensity. *Run,* I want to tell her. *You aren't wrong. She is a mood killer.*

Beth waits for me to answer, but when I don't, she takes the lead. I'm happy to give her the floor. Saves me the opportunity of saying the wrong thing. "A sponsor ensures you're acclimating to the church appropriately. They see to it that you're well cared for, and equally as important, they see to it that you understand the rules."

"Tom mentioned the rules," Mel replies, biting her lip. She leans in close and drops her voice. Also, her guard. "There seem to be a lot of them."

"Oh," Beth says. "No need to worry." She waves her off, with the flip of a wrist, like it's nothing. "You'll catch on soon enough."

I down the last of the wine, and then press my lips together. When I can manage, when the magic elixir settles in and soothes my worry, I force a smile, and I think to myself, little does she know soon enough might be too late.

CHAPTER TEN

IZZY

"Oh good, you're home," Tyler says once he's come barreling in the door. I guess I shouldn't have left it unlocked. But then, I like living on the edge.

"You," I murmur without glancing up from my laptop. He leans against the bar. I feel his eyes on me.

"I brought you a little something."

I don't look up. I don't have to. I know why he's here, and what his next move will be. Also, I'm engrossed in what I'm doing. "Is that so?"

He feigns sadness. "You don't seem very happy to see me," he says almost mockingly. "I guess I should go..."

He's trying to get me to call his bluff, but I don't bite. In the end, he doesn't care one way or the other. Actually, the more I think about it, the more I realize I have no idea what Tyler does care about. Not that I give a damn, either. It's just an observation.

I used to see him in passing in the building, coming or going, but not really see him, you know? He was always sort of just there, somewhere in the background. Until one day about seven months after Josh died, he called out for me in the hall. "I got your mail," he said, handing over a letter. When I looked down, it wasn't my name on the envelope. It was Josh's. He studied me carefully, and then he sighed like any display of emotion was more than he'd bargained for. "I'm sorry," he said. It caught me off guard.

"Everyone dies," I told him.

"Yes, about that," he replied. "I've given it some thought, and I think you need to get laid."

I managed a straight face. I perfected it over the years. And yet, it was such an off-the-cuff, unexpected remark that I didn't quite know what to do with it.

"Well," he added when I didn't respond. I studied the letters in Josh's name instead. He cleared his throat forcing me to meet his eye. "I just wanted to say I'm the man for the job...you know, if you ever need anything."

"Is there like a secret handshake or something, a smoke signal?" I asked.

"Oh," his eyes widened. "We have a smart ass," he said, eventually jutting out his bottom lip. "I like it."

I shrugged and was just about to turn and be on my merry way.

"Just leave the door ajar," he called out. "I'm home every night at seven."

I rolled my eyes, glanced down at the letter, and shook my head. "In your dreams."

"You aren't wrong about that," he said, and then he winked and went back the way he came.

I stood there and wondered how desperate I'd have to be to give in to that sort of offer.

I FOUND OUT TWO WEEKS LATER WHEN I DID ACCIDENTALLY LEAVE my door ajar. I hadn't meant to do it. Not really. I was in the process of hauling Josh's old recliner out to the dumpster. I just couldn't stand to look at the thing anymore. It was too sad. Plus,

I'd never much liked it anyway. When I came back from the dumpster, there was Tyler, sitting on my couch, legs propped up on my makeshift coffee table.

"What—"

He held his hands up. "The door was ajar."

I narrowed my eyes. "It wasn't an invitation."

"Where'd you go?"

"The dumpster."

"Ah. Well," he sighed. "It isn't wise to leave your door open. You never know who might come a-knocking."

I crossed my arms, uncrossed them, and rubbed my face with my hands. I wanted to bury my head in them forever. I wanted him to go, and yet I didn't want to feel the emptiness of being alone.

"Damn," he said, standing upright. "What a disappointment."

I looked up then and met his gaze directly. "Did you bring a condom?"

"Always," he said nonchalantly, as though he'd been expecting me to say it and then he broke out into a full grin.

I bit my lip as though I wasn't sure, when that really wasn't the case at all. I knew how I'd spend the evening if he walked out that door, and I just couldn't. "Give me thirty seconds and meet me in the bedroom," I said before making a beeline for the bathroom.

I studied my reflection in the mirror. Gave myself a pep talk. *You can do this.* It's not like it was my first foray into meaningless sex. I shouldn't have needed any of the rah-rah stuff. But it was the first time in almost a decade that any man aside from Josh would see me naked. Still. It's pretty basic, sex, the way it all works. You rub your bodies together, and with any luck you enjoy it. When you don't, pretending's not so hard. So I wasn't nervous about that. Unless he had a tiny dick, there are only so many ways to fuck it up. Pun intended.

The part I wasn't sure I could stomach was his touch. It had been seven months since anyone had touched me in an intimate way, and Tyler was a poor substitute at best. But he was living and breathing, in my living room, and willing. I didn't take him for the type to be attentive but I didn't know what I'd do if he tried the tender and sweet—let's act like this is something it isn't— route. That's not the side of the coin I like to be on.

I freshened up and then I went into the bedroom and fell back on the bed. I knew what to do. I'd done it so many times before. He came in right on schedule. I made sure the room was dark, the blackout shades closed tight. This way, I couldn't see it wasn't Josh. This way I would be better at pretending.

I shouldn't have been worried. It was mostly over before it started. He came quick that first time. There wasn't time for other positions or foreplay of any kind, and when he was done I asked him to leave.

"Just like that?" he asked.

I stared at the celling. Even in the dark I knew every crevice. "Just like that."

"I can go again—if you give me a few minutes."

"No, thank you," I said. He didn't say anything after that, not like guys would, he simply stood and dressed, and then he was gone.

But it turns out my mother had been right about feeding stray cats. He was back the night after that, and the next and the next after that. It became routine— stress relief, a workout. The sex was mediocre, like most things in my life at that point. But it was reliable.

That situation lasted for a few months, and then he met someone. Six months went by where we became nothing more than strangers. I didn't miss him. I had enough to keep me busy where missing is concerned. Still, he never looked me in the eye when I passed them in the hall.

Now, here he is, leaning against my bar like old times, back as though he'd never left.

"Didn't want to bring your girlfriend with you?" My eyes are firmly on Instalook. I prefer that reality to the one standing before me.

"I'm not into threesomes."

"That's too bad." I raise my brow and focus on the Dunns. I bet they're good at sex. I bet it's hot, adventurous. Just like them.

"Anyway, neither is she, probably. She broke up with me."

I widen my eyes but I don't meet his. "Shocker."

"Geez. What's your deal?"

"I don't have a deal."

From my periphery, I see him remove a lighter from his pocket. He's lighting a joint. His usual tactic. To guys like Tyler this counts as foreplay. It's all he knows of seduction. I wonder what Grant Dunn does for her. Actually, I don't have to wonder. I know. For them, foreplay starts long before they hit the sheets. I can see it in their photos. In the gifts he chooses.

Soon, the sweet musky scent fills the air. "Fancy a toke?"

I look up then. For the first time, I get a good look at his face. Tyler looks different. He looks heartbroken. I'd know that look anywhere. I shrug, and that's all it takes. It's an invitation. It's an acceptance. You can treat me however you want. *I'll be here.* He plops down on the couch beside me.

I don't move away.

"Whatcha lookin' at there?" he asks. I can see that he's trying to lighten the mood, but I'm not interested in talking. He passes the joint. I feel the burn on my fingertips. Sometimes pain is necessary. He stares at the screen, and then he looks up at me and smiles. "Friends of yours?"

"Not yet," I say, taking a long pull. He sticks his bottom lip out. I hold my breath. I let the smoke fill my lungs and overtake my soul.

"They seem uppity," he says, studying their faces. "Almost too happy, ya know?"

I don't know. I don't say this though. Maybe it's because we're both high, both in the safe zone, but I think I probably don't have to. And yet, I feel a bit of rage. Who is he to insult something so pure?

When I'm sufficiently high, I turn to him. "Fancy a fuck?"

He grins. "That's what I've come for."

Afterward, I bring my laptop to bed. I shuffle through photos of Grant and Josie Dunn. At some point, I look over at a sleeping Tyler, and I realize it's time to up my game.

CHAPTER ELEVEN

JOSIE

After I pick up Avery from dance, I decide to stop by that sandwich shop Grant and I visited. I know Avery won't turn down an afternoon snack, and I can't stop thinking about that Americano. The truth is, I hate Americano. What I really want, more than anything, is that sandwich I saw on the menu. Maybe it'll give me some pep; maybe it'll settle my stomach. Also, I haven't been able to put it out of my mind. It goes against my diet plan, for sure, but it costs roughly the same amount as an Americano, and that's what really matters. Plus, on the off chance I get busted, I can always say it was for Avery. I doubt Grant would check. He doesn't like to involve the kids in these things.

Either he'd believe me, or he wouldn't.

Currently, the repercussions seem too distant to think about. I'm still a bit hung over from the party and the sleeping pill Grant made me take. I knew I slipped up. I shouldn't have mentioned that I haven't been sleeping. It was a poor choice for a lie, clearly. Usually I sleep like a baby. Now, I'm groggy. Sleeping pills and alcohol don't mix. Neither do lies and my husband, but maybe that was the point. Speaking of which, I woke up to a ton of direct messages—most pictures of people consuming shellfish. The church has a way of reminding you what's important, and obviously, I've committed some sort of infraction I have yet to pay full price for.

When I pull into the parking lot, it's packed; it seems everyone on the southwest side and their mother had the same idea about coming here. I drive around in circles, and I'm about to give up when I see a sign that says there's additional parking in the back. When I pull around into the alleyway, it's mostly empty. I put the car in park and glance over at my daughter. It's probably better this way, parking back here. It's slightly less conspicuous. This is a busy shopping area, and at least back here, it lessens the chance I'll run into anyone we know. This way they won't say they saw my car. My husband's patients are everywhere, especially on this side of town, and you never know who you'll see from church. It's my job to be social. But it would be nice not to have to explain myself for once. Not to have to worry about doing or saying the wrong thing. It's a blessing and a curse, all the rules I have to remember. Like traffic laws—or any law, for that matter. What keeps you safe also limits your personal liberty.

In this case, I have a plan. It was a rough day, given everything. I spent hours scrubbing the clubhouse to perfection, my just punishment for—I'm not even sure what. Disobedience, I think. But more likely a reminder that no one is above service. No one is above God. Anyway, I did my duty, I showed that I'm willing to be put in my place when necessary, and for this my husband might let the minor infraction of slipping from my diet plan slide— if I played it just right. Checks and balances, that's what this is.

"What are we doing?" Avery asks, glancing up from her phone. She meets my eye, but her fingers never stop moving across the screen.

"Your dad and I found this coffee shop the other day," I tell her, and I have to stop and think. *How long ago was that now?* It seems that hours turn to days, and days bleed into months. I can't stop it. No one can. We wanted a slower pace of life, but I'm not sure if that's what we ended up with. I watch my daughter as she turns her attention back to her phone, texting or snapping or doing whatever it is the kids are doing these days. *What have we done?*

"Coming in?" I ask.

She doesn't glance up. "I'll wait here."

This is perfect; I won't have to involve her in my little deception. Plus, it makes sense, given her phone is glued to her face. I imagine it would be hard to walk anywhere that way. That reminds me. I pick up my phone, open my camera app, call her name, and when she looks up, she knows exactly what I'm after. She smiles. Big and wide, happily. I click and capture the moment, posting the photo to Instalook with the hashtags #qualitytime-withmygirl #howluckyamI #theygrowupsofast. Then I shove the phone in my pocket and ask her what she wants.

"Surprise me," she mutters without looking up. I tell her to lock the door, but I don't think she hears me.

"Avery!" I yell, and she looks at me then, eyes wide. She knows I do not yell. "Lock the door."

"Okayyyyy." She rolls her eyes. I shake my head and stand there outside the door for a moment until I hear the click. She's turned the speakers all the way up; She knows I hate it when she does that.

I take out my phone and check the number of likes Avery's photo has gotten. Eighty-nine so far. I shove it back in my pocket, wondering if the hashtags I used were good enough. That's when I see the girl from the coffee shop standing there, back against the wall, staring at me. She takes a drag on her cigarette and tilts her head. She's watching me. It isn't until I get a little closer that I can smell it isn't nicotine she's inhaling. She's already stubbed it out, but a scent like that lingers.

"It's you," she says, and I look behind me even though I know she couldn't possibly be speaking to anyone else.

"Excuse me?"

"Sorry," she scrambles, and I can see that she's clearly flustered.

I've busted her smoking pot, and she's only just now realized her infraction. "Excuse me. I'm...I'm... so sorry. I don't usually do this —I just—I just—"

"Don't be," I tell her, and then because I can't think of anything better to say, I add, "There wasn't any parking out front."

"Everyone comes at this time. The 3:00 p.m. crash."

"Crash?"

"Blood sugar. Or whatever it—it's a dip. People need their fix."

"Right," I say, glancing back at my SUV, wondering whether or not I'm going to have to walk around the building or whether or not there's an entrance back here.

"Tell you what," she says, reading my mind. "I'll bring your order out to your car...if you promise to keep this between us."

"You don't have to do that," I tell her, even though it's a great idea. Leaving Avery alone in an alley clearly isn't the smartest plan, seeing that I've already run into at least one person doing drugs here. I can just hear Grant now. No doubt, Avery would mention it, if she's seen. She likes to hear her father speak of the lesser people. Already, it makes her feel important. *The apple doesn't fall far from the tree.* Also, it's a deflection, and already she's good at those, too.

The girl clears her throat, that or she coughs. It's hard to tell. "It's no trouble, really."

I look over my shoulder to see if my daughter is looking my way. Of course, her head is down. Grant tells her all the time she needs to watch her posture. *Maybe we should glue that phone to your face.*

"So what'll it be? Another Americano?"

I cock my head. I'm impressed. I thought stoners were naturally forgetful. "Do you remember everyone's order?"

She shrugs.

"No," I say. "I want the Lucky's Special. And a latte. Almond milk, please."

"Okay," she nods. "But just so you know, those two don't pair so well together."

I think she's joking, but I'm not so sure.

"The latte's for my daughter."

She glances toward the car.

"But I'll have a water."

"San Pellegrino?"

I raise my brow. "How'd you know?"

She shrugs. "Just a hunch," she says and then she holds out her hand. I think she's asking for payment, so I fish a twenty from my pocket. "No," she says. "You have to shake on it."

"What am I shaking on? A hunch?"

She motions between the two of us. "To keeping secrets."

I consider her expression for a moment before eventually sliding my hand in hers. "To keeping secrets," I say.

We shake, and it seems weird but I'm in an alleyway ordering food I'm not supposed to be eating from a girl smoking pot, so weird is subjective at this point.

While I wait for her to return with my order, I scroll through and like a few dozen posts on Instalook. When she returns and hands me the bag, I carefully remove the sandwich from its wrapper. It's like unwrapping a gift marked *fragile*. I devour it within mere seconds. She leans against the wall and crosses her arms. She watches me carefully, but I'm too involved with my sandwich to care much. When I finish, I go to stuff the evidence in the bag, and see that she's added chips to my order even though I hadn't asked for them. I frown.

"It tastes better with chips," she confesses, and who am I to tell her any different?

"I haven't had potato chips in almost twenty years," I tell her. I'm pretty sure I look like a crazy person, the way I rip the bag open and gorge on them like someone who hasn't eaten in days. I know because she's still standing there watching me, although I'm not sure why. I've paid her already, and she's mentioned the shop is busy.

"Sorry," she says, as though she's read my mind. "I just wanted to see what you thought."

"It's amazing," I manage, my mouth full.

"Well then—" she half-turns. "I'd better get back."

I nod, and I keep chewing.

She turns back. "I'm Izzy, by the way."

"Josie," I say, in between fistfuls of potato chips.

"Well, Josie," she says, "It was a pleasure to meet you."

"Umhumm." I agree, but mostly I'm thinking about how I might get back here and get another of these sandwiches.

She turns and takes several steps toward the back door before she stops and turns abruptly. "I don't do this often, you know."

I swallow my mouthful. "Make women in alleyways sandwiches?"

"No," she tells me, glancing back over her shoulder. "Smoke dope."

I raise my brow. I'd already forgotten. I'm too preoccupied with this new vice of my own to consider any sins she might be harboring. "Oh," I say, waving her off. "It's our secret, remember?"

She narrows her gaze. "Funny. You know...I only smoke because it makes me hungry. Now— all I can think of is having what you're having."

"Lucky you," I say. "You work here. You get to have this anytime."

"Yes." She smiles, and it's one of Grant's. The reassuring kind. The lying kind.

CHAPTER TWELVE

IZZY

S ometimes you have to lure the fish in, and sometimes you get lucky and they come to you. I couldn't believe my eyes or my luck when I see Josie Dunn walking toward me in the alley. At first I think maybe I'm imagining it, which is why I don't immediately put out my joint. I'm not usually much of a smoker. It's Tyler. Call it peer pressure. Also, I haven't eaten in three days, and pot seems to be the only thing that helps.

I take a long pull off the joint, suck the musty smoke deep down into my lungs, into the core of me. I hold it there. She's every bit as beautiful, even though she's not wearing a dress. She looks more casual, almost relaxed. She doesn't look like the kind of woman who received hundreds of photos of shellfish—something she's highly allergic to and would mean certain death if ingested. I know, I read up on food allergies.

No, she looks like someone who has it all together. Like someone who has her emotions in check, which is one reason I don't instantly recognize it's her. This time she has on jeans and a blouse with heels, and I wonder what it must feel like to be so flawless. Scanning her Instalook again this morning, realizing more of her likes and dislikes, it finally sunk in. This time it has to be different. I realized I can't be stupid about this. I can't send immature jabs when I'm lonely or when I've had one too many. I have to be strategic. I don't want to watch from afar. Less like last time. That wasn't real. That's why it didn't last.

I want it to be like this. Up close and personal. I want her to come to me. And just like that, she has.

Already, I feel like I know her. I know she likes dinner parties and hates traffic. She doesn't hate a lot. She's not one of 'those women.' Her positive to negative ratio is roughly eleven to one.

It probably doesn't hurt that she's married to Dr. Grant Dunn, plastic surgeon extraordinaire. That part kind of surprised me; she doesn't strike me as the type who's had work done. But maybe he's just that good. They have two kids. One boy, one girl. The perfect family. She's into flowers, salads, and spin class. Typical. But there's something different there, too. For one, she doesn't try too hard. She isn't trying to get people to like her.

I can tell.

They just do.

They vacation at least twice a year: once in the winter and once in the summer. She's proud of her children, and her husband clearly adores her. It's evident in the photographs he takes. In fact, I would argue that he takes just as many as she does. An involved family man. The kind I know Josh would have been. Sure, we might not have had their money, but we could have been that happy. We were that happy. Once.

I can have that again. I just have to dig deep. That's what @liveyourbestlife224 says. Sometimes you have to dig deep. And I am. I have.

∼

"Izzzzzy," Stacey calls out the back door. The sound of her voice makes me jump. She likes to do that, draw my name out as long as she can. I don't like the way it sounds coming from her lips, but I can't exactly tell her as much—not now. Not now that @Josie_Dunn loved my sandwich. Not now that I really need this job. Not now that I know she'll be back.

"Izzy," Stacey says. "There you are." She finds me in the back, washing the last of the dishes. We have a dish washer but her kid had a thing at school tonight, some performance or something, so I said I'd finish up. I'm not supposed to be back here—I'm supposed to be off the clock, and I assume that's why Stacey's saying my name in that manner. She may have money, but that's the thing about rich people. They like to hold on to what they have.

"Where's Maria?" she asks, her eyes searching the kitchen, taking note of the fact that I am elbow-deep in dish water.

"Her kid had a thing…"

She squints as though she has no idea what I could possibly be talking about. "A thing?"

"Like a performance."

"Oh."

I don't stop washing. Maria's job isn't as easy as mine. But Stacey wouldn't know that. She wouldn't know hard labor if it struck her in the face. I know I'm considering testing my theory.

"You'd think she'd need the money."

She did need the money. She'd even said as much, when I'd suggested covering for her. I told her not to worry, and I slipped her a twenty. It was more than she would've made in the two hours she had left here, but Grant Dunn had left it in the tip jar, and I figured Maria needed it more than me. I only had one mouth to feed, and lately, barely had that.

"I don't think she was feeling well," I lie. I'm careful about it, though. It's not an outright lie. It's just my opinion, which can't be used against you the same way a real lie can.

"Oh—that's too bad. Say— I was going to ask if you wouldn't mind placing the dairy order again this week?"

I tilt my head and set the plate on the drying rack. "It's due in the morning."

She frowns. "I know. It's just that I have a date."

I want to tell her this is her problem. This is her business, not mine, and that the order is due at the same time every week. I want to tell her this will mean staying an hour even after I close up. But that's not what I say at all. I could use the money, anyhow. "Sure," I tell her, and with that she smiles sweetly. Then I watch as she turns on her heels and walks out.

"Thanks again," she calls when she reaches the counter. I listen as she gathers her things. She's happier than usual. She has the shot at the one thing money can't buy in earnest— love. For this reason alone, I know better than to engage her. I hate hearing about her dating life. It's above and beyond my pay grade. Not that she understands that. People like Stacey—rich people—hardly know boundaries.

Finally, when I've had enough pretending to busy myself in the back, when I can tell that she's heading out, I make my way to the front.

"I don't know what I'd do without you," she says, slinging her purse over her shoulder. "You're a lifesaver, I swear."

"Not really," I say. But she's already gone.

I CLEAN UP, AND THEN I PLACE THE ORDER FOR THE DAIRY, WHICH was an even bigger pain in the ass than I thought it would be. Stacey hadn't figured in that we release the pumpkin spice latte next week, and that calls for double the whip we normally order. Thankfully we aren't busy, or it would have taken me even longer, and I have to make it to the bus stop by 9:30, otherwise I have to wait a full hour for the final bus of the night to make its way back around. I'm just finishing up counting the till when I hear the doorbell chime. I look up, and I see him. Grant Dunn. He looks almost confused as he steps through the doorway, as though he's misplaced something, and he isn't sure this is where he'll find it.

"I'm sorry," he says, checking his watch and then meeting my eye. "Are you closed?"

Technically, we closed two minutes ago but I remember the twenty dollar tip and his million dollar grin and I simply say, "What can I get you?"

"I was thinking about an Americano, actually."

He smiles, and there's something in his eye that lets me know, he hasn't forgotten they aren't on the menu.

"Decaf?"

He tilts his head as though it isn't late, as though I'm crazy for the thought. "I never do things halfway."

I nod, and then I swallow hard because he's looking at me the way I've seen him look at her in the photos, and I never want it to stop. I gather the things I need and flip the espresso machine back on. It comes to life, and I busy my hands.

"Busy today?"

"Always," I say, and it isn't a lie. Today was abnormally busy. We've just gotten the first cool front of the season and suddenly everyone thinks run-of-the-mill coffee is a good idea.

"I hope you don't mind, but there's something I need to ask you..."

I look up then and meet his eye.

"It's the reason I came back, actually. I just have to know..."

I swallow hard, because his stare is burning a hole through me. I'm pretty sure in all my years in existence, no one has ever looked at me this way before. I can't speak. I can't think. Somehow I manage to lift my brow.

He waits for a second before he speaks. He holds my stare. "Who was Joshua?"

CHAPTER THIRTEEN

JOSIE

Grant leans in and releases my hair from a ponytail. He tosses the hair tie onto the bathroom counter and then meets my eye. "I missed you today," he says, as he runs his hands through my hair, fanning it out.

I study my reflection in the mirror behind him.

"All those women and you know what?"

I offer up a blank stare. It's best to let him tell me. That's how this game works.

He smirks, and I can see why my husband is so good with the women he's just mentioned. "I couldn't wait to get home to you..." he tells me. "You are so beautiful, Josie."

I lean forward and throw my arms around him. He makes me believe, even as he's adjusting my appearance to suit his tastes.

"Wow," he says. "It's good to know you feel the same way." He's playing smug, but I can see the exhaustion on his face. I can hear the weariness in his tone. Or maybe that's just what I want to hear. Maybe I want to know he's every bit as worn out as I am. Maybe if that were the case, we could slow things down a little.

I pull away and search his eyes. He looks like he used to back in residency, when the days were long, and the pay was little. Only now—the circles underneath his eyes are more apparent—the wrinkle between his brow more pronounced. Time has its way of doing that. I reach up and run my finger along the crease to smooth it out. You'd think as a plastic surgeon, that he might take care of any sign of aging. But not Grant. He says it makes him look wiser, more capable. He isn't wrong.

"Thank you for working so hard for us," I say to him, and I mean it. Despite everything that's happened, this is true. It has to be. That's why it works. I keep the emotions real.

He leans forward and plants a kiss on my forehead. Then he takes my forearms in his hands and squeezes. *This is what our life has become,* I think. Stolen moments. Bittersweet truths. He glances around me toward the door. "The kids in bed?"

"Yes," I tell him, knowing what he wants. This time I want it too.

"Perfect. Let's have a bath."

I don't want to undress in front of him. I'm afraid he'll know what I've done. In my mind, I imagine that he'll see the grease from those potato chips glistening on my thighs.

"I'm a plastic surgeon," he told me once after Avery was born. "It's my job to notice small subtleties. What kind of doctor would I be if I couldn't calculate exact measurements on sight?" I was having a hard time getting back in shape. It's the only time he's asked me to go under the knife. He knows I'm terrified of needles. This, in and of itself, was enough to push me in the right direction.

That's when I learned the secrets of dropping weight quickly. They want you to believe that veggies and exercise will do the trick. And maybe they're right. But starving yourself is easier. Also, if given the choice between broccoli and nothing, I'd just as soon go with nothing.

"In you go," he orders once the tub is half full. He eyes me from head to toe. "You must be exhausted."

"I am," I say, but I don't immediately budge. I don't want to undress. I'm hoping he'll leave me, even though I know he won't.

"I was thinking," he tells me. He's sitting on the side of the tub, removing his cufflinks. "That maybe it's time to update this bathroom."

I watch as he unbuttons his shirt. It was a clinical day, which means he spent most of the day alternating between consultations and follow-ups. It's surgery my husband prefers, and already I know the kind of day he had will make him edgy, restless.

"A remodel?" My husband likes to keep me occupied. He likes to ensure I don't have a moment of peace.

"It's a bit dated, don't you think?"

I laugh. "This bathroom is less than five years old…"

"Yes, but things move faster these days. Plus, we can afford it, and it'd be nice to have a change of scenery—tell me you disagree."

"No," I say, glancing around the space. "I see your point."

"Beth said the clubhouse looks absolutely stunning."

My face reddens. There's something about Beth knowing that I've spent the greater part of my day scrubbing floors that bothers me. What bothers me worse is that my husband has spoken to her about it. I'm careful not to let it show, because I know if I can keep him talking, if I can keep the mood light, then it will divert attention away from other things. "I'm glad she liked it."

I begin to undress. "How was your day?"

"Tiring," he tells me. "But good. Next month will be a busy one."

I raise my brow. My husband's business is booming most of the year. Just before the holidays, even more so. People rush in to have their inadequacies tweaked before they have to face them at family gatherings.

"Wonderful."

He gives me the once over, but I can see his mind is elsewhere. "I was thinking we should get away soon," he mentions without looking at me. "I think you need it."

"A remodel and a vacation," I say jokingly. He cocks his head to the side. "That sounds like a great idea," I tell him, but as the words ooze out into the space between us, I can see we both know it's a lie. I signed an agreement prohibiting this. I wait for him to remind me. He doesn't. Not now. It probably helps that I'm naked and bath water doesn't ask permission to turn cold.

He motions me forward, and then steps in after me. We take our usual positions, him in back, me facing opposite, the back of my head resting against his chest. "Why do I get the feeling you aren't being honest with me, Josie?"

"I am being honest. I think a vacation sounds like a great idea."

He smooths the hair on my head. He runs his fingers through it. He always finds the knots. "And yet?"

"And yet—the very idea of putting it all together feels overwhelming. Especially now. We have a lot going on. The kids have a lot going on..."

"It sounds like I come in last on that list of yours."

I shake my head. "You don't."

He yanks the knot loose. I flinch. He cups my breast. Satisfied, his hand trails lower. I'm not in the mood but it won't change things. "Prove it," he says, pushing my head down, and so I do.

"IS THERE SOMETHING BOTHERING YOU?" GRANT ASKS AS I towel off.

My eyes water. "No. Why?"

"You just didn't seem as enthusiastic as you normally are."

"I'm just tired, that's all."

"I don't think you're taking good enough care of yourself Jos—"

I shrug. It's the wrong move and I instantly realize the mistake. My husband doesn't like nonchalance.

"Step on the scale," he motions. "I think we should take a look."

My eyes dart toward the mirror. "It's not time for my weigh-in..."

"I'm worried about you," he says. Clearly, he's going to call my bluff. "I know you have a lot on your plate."

"I said I'm fine."

"Yes, but preventative care is the most important kind."

I stand there for a moment, hands at my sides. We're eye to eye, toe to toe. Tears prick my eyelids but I refuse to let him see me cry. "I'm not one of your patients, Grant."

"I know. You're my wife," he says, resting his hand on my lower back motioning me forward. "The most important thing in my whole world."

Eventually, I step on the scale.

"Hmmm," he murmurs, reading the number. "You're ten ounces over."

I throw my head back, stare at the ceiling, and then let out a long heavy sigh.

He seems to think for a moment, but it's an act, he knows just what he wants to say. He's making me sweat it out. Finally, he exhales loudly. "But then, your period is coming soon."

"Like I said, I'm fine." I step off the scale and glare at his reflection in the mirror. "I'm just retaining water."

He rubs at his jaw and then stops abruptly. He runs his hands over my body. He's inspecting me the way he does his patients. I stand there, naked and humiliated. Finally, he stops and takes a step back. "I want you to see Beth tomorrow. She tells me you aren't sleeping, which is interesting..."

I slip my robe on. "I'm fine, Grant."

He grabs my forearm and looks me directly in the eye. "I mean, to have to learn about my wife's sleeping habits from Beth?"

"It was just an excuse I came up with on the fly. You know how Beth is. Always making mountains out of molehills."

"Yes, I do know how Beth is," he tells me condescendingly. "She and I both agree an audit would do you good."

"I don't need an audit."

"Don't question me, Josie. Not after this." He points toward his dick and then he looks up at me. "You know how hard I work for us, and the best you can offer at the end of a long day is a mediocre performance and obstinance?"

I swallow hard.

"You know I'm not supposed to talk about these things but... you need to know this...you're sponsoring Tom's new wife for a reason. I need to know you understand what's at stake here, Josie."

I think long and hard about what I'm going to say next, and I steady my tone before I speak. "You're right," I say. "I understand." And in that moment, I think I'm beginning to.

CHAPTER FOURTEEN

IZZY

Josie Dunn posted a picture of new running shoes to Instalook this morning. *Isn't my husband thoughtful?* she wanted to know, and clearly, the answer is yes. Now, my most pressing dilemma appears to be that I need new shoes. Mine were worn out anyhow, and wow—she's right. That man really knows his shoes. Instantly, I Google the brand and try to find out how I might get them, too. Funny thing, I'm not even a runner. But if I had those shoes, and the opportunity to get a body like Josie Dunn, I just might be willing to give it a go. Who knows? A bit of exercise might even do me good. Finally, I find the shoes and order me a pair. They aren't cheap, not that I expected as much. You get what you pay for. And if I want the kind of life the Dunns have, then I have to play the part.

Hard work pays off. Or internet shopping. Same difference. An hour later she posts a shot of herself at a trail not far from Lucky's with the caption *Breaking them in.*

I glance up at the clock, and I tell Stacey I'm taking a break. She doesn't look at me funny, not like she should, because Stacey is clueless and wouldn't know serendipity if it smacked her in the face. Trust me, I've thought about it. She's still crying over her date, the guy who hasn't called. Needless to say, she isn't good with signs. She should be out hunting her next prey, I mean, date. But Stacey's domesticated. Me, I'm working on it.

PEOPLE ARE PREDICTABLE. UNTIL THEY AREN'T. THIS IS THE BEST time to make your move. When they least expect it. I've never seen Josie Dunn post a picture from this trail before. This run-in will be perfect. She won't be expecting to see me here. Better yet, she won't be expecting *not* to see me here.

I'm not exactly dressed in workout gear, but this is Austin, so basically anything goes. Also, I'm in luck because the photo she posted shows me two things: her surroundings—A.K.A pretty much her exact location— and what she was wearing. Now, I know what to look for to find her. Even so, it takes me two tries to get her attention. The first time she's too busy staring at her phone to notice when I drop my keys right in front of her. She sort of glances up when I lean down to retrieve them, but I can see that she doesn't really see me because I can also see that she's replying to Instalook comments with people over her shared love of running. I don't miss the irony. She's not even running. She's sitting on a bench. And this is a prime example of why people don't have real friends anymore.

The second attempt, I make sure to get her to notice me. I don't just drop my keys. I drop my whole body. It's less dramatic than it sounds. I'm practically a professional. My best friend and I, we used to do this thing where we'd pretend to fall down in order to get sympathy from people, which is how I learned the tricks of the trade. My friend once earned herself an ice-cream cone. Me, I got free rides when my mother didn't show and my first experience with the likes of the Dunns of the world. I've had plenty of experience since then. But you never forget your first time. *Just let yourself fall. It's okay if it hurts.*

"Oh my gosh," Josie Dunn says, reaching out. She tries to catch me, but not hard enough. It's okay though. It's better this way. Guilt does amazing things to people. She looks at me sideways. "Are you okay?"

I squint into the sunlight. She looks like an angel. But I bet she isn't. I grunt, and I clutch my ribs. "Yeah," I wince. "I will be."

"Here—" she says. "Let me help you."

"It's okay," I counter, brushing myself off. "I'll manage."

She eyes me intently. My shades fell off on my way down. "Wait," she gasps. "I know you. From the coffee shop."

I search her face. I narrow my eyes. I pretend. It's fun to fuck with people. "Coffee shop?"

She looks confused. "We met in the alley…yesterday."

I cock my head slightly to give the impression I'm thinking hard.

She exhales slowly. I want to hate her. She's just so beautiful and so concerned that I feel sorry for her instead. "But you probably see a ton of people…"

When I don't answer, her expression grows more concerned.

She chews at her bottom lip. I watch as she shifts her weight from foot to foot. She glances right and then left. Josie Dunn is looking for a way out. She's looking for someone else to take responsibly for the predicament she's found herself in. People like her always do. It comes natural to them. "Do you know what day it is?"

I close one eye and focus hard on her face, her eyes specifically. "Monday?"

She shakes her head slowly. "No," she says, sucking her bottom lip in further. "Is there someone I can call?"

I hold up one finger and reach in for the energy bar from my pocket. I tear the wrapper and stuff a piece into my mouth. Once I've chewed and swallowed, I start to take a second bite but she looks so stunned, so helpless, I give up the act. "I'm just fucking with you," I say, and I bet no one speaks to Josie Dunn like that.

"I know what day it is. And I remember you. You like Americanos."

"Oh," she says, and I see relief. Her body visibly relaxes. The creases around her eyes soften. "How strange running into you here…"

I laugh at her pun. She doesn't get it. "Not that strange. I walk this route every day."

She juts her bottom lip out.

"Nice kicks by the way…"

She glances down at her shoes. "Thanks."

"They're very clean…"

She blushes. "Forgive me," she says, extending her hand. I've embarrassed her by pointing out my position. I'm beneath her. Not just figuratively, but literally. I'm still on the ground, inept and clumsy. She smiles, and she towers above me, giving the impression that she has the upper hand. Women like Josie Dunn like the upper hand and still they pretend they're embarrassed by having it. "Here," she tells me, shaking her head. "Let me help you."

I take the hand she's offered, and I'm surprised by how soft it is. Like it's never seen a hard day's work in its life. "Sorry," I offer. "I'm new at this running thing."

When we're eye to eye, she checks her phone. I can see the notifications lighting up her screen. "Yeah," she says, smiling at her phone. "It's been awhile for me too…"

"Say," I press my lips together and rub at my knee. "Why don't you come by Lucky's later?"

She's still staring at the phone. I deepen my voice. "Coffee on me. Or a sandwich, if you'd like." She looks up then. I shrug like it's nothing. "That way I can thank you properly for saving my life."

"I didn't save your life…I hardly helped you to your feet."

"No," I promise. "It's the low blood sugar thing. If you hadn't been here…"

Her brow furrows. I study her face. I want to hate her. I want her to ask me to dinner. I want to be best friends. It doesn't make any sense. These things never do.

"If you hadn't been here, well, who knows if someone would have stopped. You know how people are these days..."

I see something in her demeanor shift. She falters momentarily, lets her guard down. Josie Dunn wants somebody to save.

She narrows her gaze. "That reminds me," she smiles. "Do you go to church? "

LATER IN THE DAY, AFTER I HAVE AN INVITATION TO ATTEND CHURCH with the Dunns, well technically just Josie Dunn, but still. It's more than I could have hoped for, even just this morning. Fine, I'll admit it. The invitation has taken me a quick minute to reconcile — I'd hardly taken them for the religious type— but I guess it's nice to be surprised every now and then.

I go back to work, and all the while, I hope Josie will change her mind and take me up on that coffee. Every time the bell rings, I pray I'll look up and see her standing there. Every. Single. Time. I don't know what it is about her. I just know I have to see her again. And soon.

As I make my billionth latte of the afternoon, I hope she misses my face as much as I miss hers. She's not here though. So I guess she doesn't. But it's okay, I guess. Luckily, I don't have to miss her for long. Josie Dunn posts a picture of her and some leggy blonde woman at lunch with the hashtag #herestofriends. I study the photo carefully. I wish I were at home, where I could see it on a bigger screen than just my phone. Oh, well. At least this gives me something to look forward to.

I zoom in. She's changed her clothes and fixed her hair. The two of them look smug, smiling at the camera. They're dressed casually, in flowy tops, tight jeans and kitten heels. Also in a way that tells you their brand of casual is one that you could never afford. When I get a closer look, I can see they're enjoying the most gorgeous salad I've ever seen with the hashtag #NewHope #blessed. The post gets 837 likes within an hour. This bums me out. I was wrong. I could never actually be Josie Dunn. One, I'd have to land a man like that, one that cares about surprises and shoes, and two, I don't even think I know 837 people.

I breathe a sigh of defeat. Maybe if I can't be Josie, I can at least be her sidekick. Anyway, it shouldn't be too hard to assume the position. Her friend has nothing on her in terms of charisma. But even I have to admit, she is beautiful. I flip the camera on my phone and study myself. I tussle my hair. *With a bit of money and a little work, you could be that.*

I WASN'T GOING TO EAT ANYTHING FOR LUNCH BUT SUDDENLY A salad sounds good. I zoomed in on their food, and I did my best to replicate what I saw. In fact, I'm eating it, forcing myself to like the taste of lettuce and health, when the doorbell chimes. I look up and just like that, my unspoken prayers have been answered. It's not Josie Dunn.

It's better.

It's her husband.

I don't know how I do it, but it seems the more I familiarize myself with them online, the more they seem to pop into my life when I least expect it. It's like magic. Only not fake.

"Hello." Grant greets me with the enthusiasm only a man of his stature can have. His voice is deep, and in it there's something else, something beyond confidence. Something I can't place. This time he's in scrubs and one of those funny surgical hats, and it makes him look younger, much younger. I look down at my attire, and I curse myself for not putting in more effort. *What a fool you are, thinking you could be like her. Look at him. He'd never want you. A glorified waitress, of all things.*

I drop my fork and rest my hands on my hips. I don't like looking at something I can't have. I need to feel the rage. I need to feed it. "Let me guess. You want an Americano?"

He shakes his head. "No."

I smooth my apron.

"Wow," he says eyeing my food. "That looks good."

I bite my lip and wonder if he'll notice the similarity between his wife and I, even if there's only this one.

If he does, he doesn't say anything. He scans the menu. "My wife mentioned she had a sandwich here..." he says, trailing off. I watch him intently. My mouth goes dry. I fumble for words. None come to mind.

Eventually, he places the menu on the counter and he looks me up and down. "Do you remember my wife?"

It must be a trick question. I have to say yes. I'd be willing to bet they're the kind of couple who tells each other everything. She probably sent him to collect the freebies I offered. He doesn't wait for me to answer. He smiles and it's genuine. He likes thinking of her too. "The original orderer of the Americano?"

"Sure," I say, heat rising in my belly. "She ordered the special."

"I bet she did." He grins at the thought, and I can see his love for her in his upturned lips. "I think I'll have one of those—wait... you know what? Make it two."

How nice that he wants the same, I think as I type the order in.

"She's always appreciated a good surprise."

"Do you want chips?" I ask dismissively. I could just put them in the bag, but with him it seems different. With him, it seems like going out of your way might have the opposite effect.

He raises his brow. "She had chips too, did she?"

"Yes," I tell him and I feel something building. Sadness. Dizziness. Pure unadulterated longing. I guess she didn't tell him about me, about our meeting in the alley or in the park. I sigh. "I remember that she loved them."

His eyes widen. "Sure," he smirks. "Chips would be great." The look on his face is to die for. "Hey, why not throw in a double order."

I don't tell him she won't need his surprise because she's already been to lunch and she had a salad. I can't say that, even though I want to. It's too early in the game for thoughtless mishaps.

Anyway, he'd know if he'd checked her Instalook account. Instead, he's focused on me. He watches closely as I ring up the order. *You really ought to be more thorough, Grant Dunn. But then you're a doctor, and you're probably pretty busy. In fact, I know you are.*

"Excuse me?"

I eye him confused.

"You just said, I know you are..."

"No I didn't."

He cocks his head. "I'm pretty sure you called me... Josh."

"I was singing," I say pointing to the sound system. "I'm not very good. Obviously," I laugh. "Not if people think I'm mumbling."

He starts to speak, and then he presses his lips together and shakes his head slightly. "Well, practice makes perfect."

I nod. *That it does.* I know. I studied the images of the before and afters on his website. I'm a sucker for that sort of thing, and I wonder what I might look like with a few enhancements. I wonder if he finds that kind of perfection attractive. Of course, he does. Look at his wife. I want to ask him about his work. But I've found it's better to figure out things organically, so I finish making his wife's sandwich instead.

THAT NIGHT AS I'M WALKING HOME AFTER MY SHIFT, simultaneously scrolling Instalook and imagining the conversation that could have been, I see headlights circle around, and something in the pit of my stomach stirs.

"Izzy?" I hear a voice call in the dark. I know it instantly.

I crane my neck into the darkness to make sure I'm not hearing things.

"Hey," he says when my eyes lock in on his. The gravel crunches beneath the tires as he pulls the car slowly along side me. "Need a ride?"

You need to be more careful, Izzy. Josh's voice rings in my ears. I don't want to listen, but I know better. It won't go away. It refuses to die like the rest of him. "That's okay," I say. "I don't have too far to go."

"Seriously," he counters. "It seems we're headed in the same direction. It's really no trouble."

Don't do it, Izzy. Smart people don't get in the car with strangers. But Grant Dunn isn't a stranger.

I shake my head. "I'm good, really."

"Izzy," he says, and I have to admit I do like the way my name sounds coming from his lips. "I don't want to sound overprotective, but you shouldn't be walking alone after dark."

I shrug. He sounds like Josh now, and something in me softens. I want to tell him I wouldn't be walking if we hadn't had those teenagers linger at closing time. I wanted to tell him that as they finally left in their fancy cars and I locked up, I realized I'd already missed my bus. "Come on," he urges, coming to a complete stop. "It's nothing, really."

Hardly, I want to tell him. But instead, I simply nod and walk around to the passenger door. My breath quickens. I might hyperventilate. My head is spinning. I'm wracking my brain, trying to figure out how to get him to drop me off somewhere—anywhere—other than my dumpy apartment complex. Although, everywhere on my side of town is too shabby for the likes of Grant Dunn, so even if I could come up with something on the fly, I don't know where that might be.

He looks over at me. "This side of town always makes me a bit nostalgic," he tells me, coolly. "It's where Josie and I first lived together. Back when I was pre-med."

"Oh," I say, and I'm shocked. My breath steadies now that I can see he's willing to let me in. Not just in his car, either.

I look over. He's already looking. "You remind me a bit of her."

His expression catches me off guard. I feel dizzy at the thought that I remind him of someone as brilliant as his wife.

"She's gorgeous," I tell him. It sounds silly, girlish, once it's out of my mouth and out in the open. Instantly I wish I could take it back.

"So are you," he murmurs. My cheeks warm. My whole body feels like it's floating. I'm not in the car; I'm above it, looking down on me, a different, luckier version of myself. Suddenly, he brings me back. He places his hand on mine, and I have to say, I hadn't seen that coming.

CHAPTER FIFTEEN

JOSIE

"I met someone," I tell Beth over a salad I practically inhale. I notice she barely touches hers. Not at first. This is an audit, and audits are designed to get to the heart of the matter. She wants to squeeze as much out of me as she can. I'll want to be very careful about what I say. I learned this the hard way. "Anyway," I add nonchalantly. "I invited her to our meeting on Thursday. I think she has potential…"

Beth's expression is unreadable. "It's been so long since you brought someone in," she tells me, her eyes wide. "She *must* be special."

"It hasn't been that long," I say. But then I consider the last person, and I realize she's right. "I've never been as good as you at it. But I do try."

"Look at you, kissing up." She frowns. "That's not your style."

"What? I thought you wanted honesty." I lay my hands flat on the table. "I thought that's why we're here."

"Grant is worried about you, Josie."

"That is not your concern."

She doesn't blink. "It's your husband's concern, which makes it the church's concern."

I look away. "It shouldn't be anyone's concern."

"You're not sleeping. You're over your weight limit. You're speaking ill of New Hope to new members—Tom's wife, of all people. I mean, come on, Josie. Of course, this is a concern. It's out of character."

It doesn't matter what I say. So I start with the obvious. "It's just been difficult…since June died."

"For all of us," she agrees. Then she seems to consider what to say next. "But we have to move on, Josie. June would want that."

"Well, Tom certainly has. Moved on."

Her lips fold inward. "What's he supposed to do?"

"I don't know—grieve."

"People grieve differently, Jos— particularly men."

I figured Beth would say that. She excuses the opposite sexes' shortcomings like nobody's business.

"You're right," I tell her. "Maybe I have been thinking about it wrong. I think I just needed a fresh perspective. I think June's death has reminded me of my own mortality. It's scary, you know. To realize that we're all going to die. "

She nods. This is what she wants to hear.

She stabs her fork into a tomato. She's half-finished with her salad, meanwhile, I'd like to order another. "And the weight gain?"

"I'm getting my period."

I watch as she stuffs the tomato in her mouth. She chews slowly. I feel my fight or flight reflex kick in, and it takes a lot to stuff it back down. "You know women have to allow for these things."

"Yes," I agree. "I've been weak."

"We'll need to advance your workout schedule."

"I'm already doing six days a week."

"Now, you'll do seven. Sometimes it just takes a little extra to get the edge, you know."

I don't say anything. I sip my water. Sometimes you have to let things run their course.

"I have some audio files I'll be emailing you. We'll need you to listen and report back your interpretations."

"What kind of files?"

She twists her fork around in her salad. It looks like she's picking at a wound, seeing how much she can make it bleed. "You know, the usual," she says, and she places the fork on the table. I look on as she takes her straw between her fingertips. She dips it further into her water and then slowly pulls it out. She stabs at her lemon. I want to take the glass and hurl the water at her. I see it in slow motion. She smiles. "Just a reinforcement of the rules. Excellence training. That sort of thing."

Excellence training. This is what Beth calls hours and hours of recorded audio of her voice. "Okay," I say finally. "Is that it?"

"Well, there is one more thing…"

"What's that?"

I watch as she reaches into her purse and fishes something out. She places the bottle on the table like it's nothing.

"I don't need medication, Beth."

"It's just a little something to help you get back on track."

"I'm fine."

"Take the pills, Jos. You'll feel better."

I take the bottle and toss it into my bag.

"Oh," she says. "And I can't wait to meet this friend of yours. I'm sure she's going to fit right in."

I smile, but the way she says it I can tell, she's being condescending. We both remember the last person I recruited, and that one didn't turn out so well.

I'M SURPRISED TO FIND GRANT'S CAR IN THE DRIVE WHEN I ARRIVE home. He's never home in the middle of the day. I wonder if Beth put him up to this. I wonder if they've already spoken about lunch. My breath catches for a moment. Maybe I wasn't as convincing as I thought. I turn off the ignition and stare at the garage door. I'm being silly. I know how much my husband's time is worth. I know how busy his schedule is. If he's home, it's not because of something I said over lunch.

When I enter the house, I see the spread on the table, and I realize I'm right. I know why he's here. He knows I lied.

He has a meal for two laid out on the table when surely he's aware I've already eaten. He's in the kitchen. I can hear the water running. I get the urge to turn and tiptoe out the front door.

"Oh good," I hear him call out before I can force myself to make a move. "You're here."

"What are you doing home?" I ask, careful of my tone.

He dries his hands on a dishtowel and then meets my eye. "I wanted to bring you lunch."

I furrow my brow. I tell myself I won't give into him that easily. "But you knew I was meeting with Beth. Doctor's orders, remember?"

This is apparently the wrong thing to say. "So what. It's a gift, Josie," he tells me motioning toward the dining room. "Sit."

"Grant, I'm not hungry."

"You will eat with me," he says matter of factly.

"I've just eaten with Beth."

"So—all of a sudden you care about moderation? I don't get you. Why start now?"

"Grant—I can explain."

He shakes his head. "You heard me," he points at the table. "I want to see you eat both mine and yours."

"I can't eat all that," I say incredulously.

I should have stopped there. I should have quit while I was ahead. *Never be disagreeable.* I should have picked up the sandwich and taken a bite, apologized. *Diffuse the situation. Make your husband feel at ease in his home. This is your job.*

I take a deep breath in. He walks over to me, his eyes heavy, his expression blank. "I'm sorry," I say finally. "I shouldn't have—"

It's too late. He cuts me off by grabbing a fistful of my hair and drags me over to the table. He shoves my head down. "You will eat every bite."

I glance up at the clock. I have to pick up Avery soon, and I can't afford for this to escalate. I take one bite and then another. I chew slowly. He tightens the grip he has on my hair. "Do you really think I have all day to sit here and babysit you?"

He shakes my head for me using the tight grip he has on my hair. I swallow quickly and take another bite.

"Chew faster," he orders. I hear the anger in his voice. He doesn't yell. He doesn't have to. "You have really let me down this time, Josie."

"I'm sorry," I say.

"Why are you talking?" he asks. "You should be eating."

I try to shift a bit, to get my bearings. I am bent at the waist, and this makes it hard. I straighten my legs, or at least I try. I'm afraid my knees are going to buckle, that they'll give out, and all I'll have is my husband holding me up by my hair.

"Faster!" he orders. I shove more food in. "I have to get back to work," he tells me. "I like it better there. You know, *there* women actually care about their bodies...I enjoy spending time with people who care about their health."

"I do care."

"Maybe," he laughs. "But what you lack is discipline, Josie. You know, real effort."

I feel a sense of dread. He's not going to let up.

"Look at this," he says, swinging my head wildly. "Look at what I provide for you. And for what? For nothing. You don't deserve this," he chuckles. "If there was a grand prize for laziness...surely you'd take first place."

I don't respond. It's better that way.

Eventually, I succeed at getting one sandwich down and half of the other before I literally cannot eat anymore.

He sighs. "If you don't eat the rest of that, there will be severe consequences, Josie." He's growing more impatient. "Do you understand what I mean?"

I take another bite, but I can't make myself chew. I close my eyes. *You can do this.*

He kicks the back of one knee, causing it to buckle. It's not a hard blow, not so much that it hurts, anyway; it's just hard enough to make my leg give out. Just enough to make me rely on him for balance. It's what he's best at. I'm twisting and turning, trying to steady myself, when I feel the sharp, cool metal against my back.

"Eat it, I said!"

I do as he says. I hear him place the knife or scalpel or whatever he has on the table. Then I manage to stuff the rest of the sandwich down as well as a fistful of chips, before my gag reflex kicks in. With one hand he lifts my head up and with the other he takes a fistful of chips and forces them into my mouth. I manage, but when he tries to force more in, I vomit all over him and the table. I'm not used to consuming that much food. My stomach can't handle it. Tears stream down my cheeks.

"Now look what you've done."

I'm sobbing, and I'm choking, and things have never looked this hopeless. *There's no coming back from this.*

"Hmmm," he says, taking his phone from his pocket. He selects his angle, twisting me by my hair, forcing my face toward the vomit, and he snaps a picture. "Why don't you post that on the internet?"

I feel dizzy.

He laughs. Vomit burns my nostrils.

The smell is horrific.

"Now—take a bite, say you're sorry, and this can all be over…"

I refuse without words. He shoves my head down until my face rests against the vomit. It's chunky, warm and wet.

He pushes on my cheek forcing my head to turn. "DO IT."

I'm sobbing, but eventually I open my mouth and suck in the

smallest amount possible. Still enough that I know it will satisfy him.

He exhales loudly and lets go of my hair. "That a girl."

I try to stand then. I intend to run and keep running. Maybe I'll never come back. He holds me down. "Are you going to lie to me again?"

"No," I promise. But even I don't believe myself.

I feel the cold, sharp edge rest against my skin. I squeeze my eyes shut. I feel warm liquid running down my back.

"Jesus, Josie. Look at you—" he says, mockingly. "Always adding more work for me."

My eyes burn, my throat is raw. I feel nothing.

He raises the scalpel to my face at eye level. "Tell me—" he scoffs. "What am I supposed to do with something I can't fix?"

CHAPTER SIXTEEN

IZZY

I don't ask, but the next night after work Grant Dunn is there in the parking lot waiting to drive me home. I watch him under the soft glow of the street lamps. He looks tired. "You don't have to do this," I say, leaning against the passenger door, thinking it shouldn't be this easy. "I can take the bus."

"It's cold out."

I roll my eyes playfully. "You're the one out here with your windows down."

"I like the cold. But you. Well, you don't even have a proper jacket." I glance down at my outfit. The one I copied from @fashionistaforver777. It arrived yesterday, and I wore it today. Just in case. He's right. A cool front blew in this afternoon, and I hadn't factored that in. I hadn't thought to bring a jacket.

"This is Texas. Not Alaska. I'll survive."

He holds his hands up as though I need to say no more. "I was on my way home from rounds. It's no biggie."

He shifts his gaze and stares straight ahead for a moment before looking over at me once again. Then he raises his brow. "Plus, if something were to happen, how else am I supposed to get an Americano in this town?"

I laugh and let his dark sense of humor fill my soul.

"Come on," he ushers me. "It shouldn't be this hard to give a lady a ride. Get in."

I do as he says. Then I thank him and tell him I appreciate how considerate he is.

"Like I said. It's nothing."

This must be how his wife feels. Cared for. Grateful.

I buckle my seatbelt. He turns to me and hands me his phone. When I glance down I see that he has his contacts pulled up. My name is typed in. I look up at him. His expression is unreadable. I take a deep breath. I tell myself to play it cool. Still, I feel the blood rushing to my cheeks, and I know I'm busted. I curse myself for being as transparent as they come. I will myself to calm down, to relax, but it's not as easy as it seems.

It feels amazing—on another level— to see my name on Grant Dunn's phone. I have to admit, something shifted when he reached for my hand. I was disappointed. I thought he and his wife were happy.

Don't get me wrong—it wasn't that a small part of me didn't want it to happen. I did. What I don't understand, and what I am determined to find out, is why. Why would he go and mess up a good thing?

Surely, he wouldn't hurt Josie that way. I feel so conflicted. It's like my heart and my mind are duking it out. All day they've played tug-o-war with each other to see which one will come out victorious. Now, we're down to the final round.

I frown at the thought of either winning, and he takes notice. I'm an open book.

"What's wrong?"

I didn't think you were the type to be unfaithful. "Do you think true love exists?"

He glances at me furtively, and I can see that he's not thrown off by my question. He's giving it careful consideration. "Well," he answers finally, eyes straight ahead. "I think that depends on one's definition of true love."

Maybe Tyler is right. Maybe it doesn't exist. I don't say anything.

"So, let's hear it. What do you think it is?"

I laugh. "I have no idea."

"Sure you do."

I stare out the passenger window, and I don't say anything for a few moments. "I thought, when I saw you and your wife that day you came into Lucky's," I confess. "I thought, now there's true love."

"I do love my wife. So—you weren't wrong."

"No," I tell him half-grateful, half-irritated. "I didn't think I was."

It didn't take long for me to fall from my high horse. Josie posted a picture last night on Instalook of Grant with their daughter, together, lying on the sofa, his hand on hers. Hashtag #greatestthingever. Then I remembered how childish I am. I remembered what he does for a living. Touching people, making them feel beautiful, making them feel *seen*—that's his job. His hand on mine meant nothing more.

This was soothing and hurtful, all the same. I'm not special, and Josie Dunn is who she says she is on the internet. They do have true love.

I know because I scoured Josie's page from beginning to end. Twelve hundred and ninety-two posts. I read and studied them all. Every minor detail. I had to know for sure I don't have a shot. I had to know I'm right. I had to know, before I go any further, before I get in too deep. I had to know I'm not missing anything. I had to know she really is every bit as perfect as she seems.

In the end, I didn't find anything to the contrary. Just yesterday, she posted a photo of herself volunteering at an old folks home, and I realized she is the real deal. I know for sure if I had her life, I wouldn't be spending my time with crusty old people in places that smell like stale piss. Not me. I'd be hitting up the mall.

I'd be traveling. Josie Dunn is something else. She's on another level. Not only is she more attractive than the rest of us, she's selfless, too, and this makes me despise her even more. But it also makes me like her, and that's the scary part. I remember what happened the last time I got too close.

"Thanks for your number," Grant says jarring me, bringing me back to the here and now where I belong. I nod, and then he turns on some melancholic song I've never heard before, and I wonder if he's playing it for me. I wonder if it's a message. He gets me. *This can never work,* he's telling me. *You are not her, and I could never love you.*

Eventually, he pulls up to the apartment complex across the street from the one I actually inhabit. It's only slightly nicer. When he puts the car in park, I hand him his phone. His hand brushes mine, and it hits me in the pit of my stomach. I look away. He never does. "This way," he says, tilting it in my direction, "If I need a quick fix I can just text, and you can have my coffee ready. Or— if you're in need of a ride, well— now you have a direct line."

"Thanks," I say. My mouth twists, and I don't mean for it to happen. It's just that when he speaks, it's so slow and deep. The tone of his voice combined with the smooth bravado I hear as words drip from his lips make the simplest of niceties sound so sexual. So inviting.

But maybe that's just wishful thinking.

I frown. I don't want to want Grant Dunn. I want him, and I hate myself for it. That's what they don't tell you. It's painful to want something you can't have.

My expression doesn't go unnoticed.

"Iz—" he says, shortening my name the way Josh used to. He tilts his head and I look up at him. "Can I call you that?"

I shake my head slowly.

"You frown like you're an imposition. But you're not. You're my friend."

I don't say anything in response, because I don't know what to say. I don't know why someone like Grant Dunn would want to be friends with someone like me. I don't know why I always have to want things I can never have.

Thankfully, I get my answer, because in addition to being handsome and successful, kind and perfect, apparently he's telepathic, too.

"From the first moment I heard the passion in your voice when you mentioned Josh's name, I knew I had to know more. I knew instantly that you were the kind of friend I needed in my life. Loyalty is hard to come by, Izzy," he says. His eyes are sad when he says it, and this makes me sad too. "But then, I'm sure you know that."

"Yes," I reply, and I think I do know.

He shifts in his seat and positions his body in my direction. "Speaking of which, you never told me about Josh. Nothing— other than he was your husband— I would like to hear more sometime."

"I—"

"Not now," he says. "Sometime when we have more time together."

I swallow hard, and I'm glad he says that because I wasn't prepared to hear Josh's name, much less speak it myself.

"That would be good," I say, and for the first time I realize Grant Dunn is the perfect confidant. He seems like someone I might want to tell about Josh.

THREE NIGHTS LATER I'M WALKING HOME AGAIN. IT'S THE WEEK before finals, and the teenagers pretend to be studying at Lucky's, or at least that's what they tell their parents, when really they're just fucking off.

It's cold out, but not frigid. Lucky's was slammed today, and my back aches from being on my feet all day.

Originally, I typed out a text to Grant to ask if he might give me a ride. But then I thought better of it and deleted the text. I don't want to be the kind of person that asks people for rides, much less someone like Grant Dunn.

We might be friends, but even I know there's a limit to friendship. I'm aware that he has more important things to do. In the end, I'm glad I deleted the text, because when I open up Instalook, I quickly learn he isn't on his way home from rounds. He and Josie are at some fancy party, and what a fool I would have felt like had I sent that text.

I study the photo carefully. I stop just so I can have another look. Josie is wearing a deep burgundy dress. It's backless and as usual she looks radiant. Grant dons a tuxedo, and in the photo she's looking up at him. She's blushing, and in her eyes there's complete admiration. I feel a sharp pain in the pit of my stomach. I don't know what it would be like to know happiness like that. But I think I used to, once upon a time.

I go home, and I feed Josh's damned cat, and I plop down on the bed. I don't even bother to change out of my work clothes. I'm too exhausted to take another step. But I don't sleep. I lay there and try to imagine all of the times I might have felt the way Josie felt in that Instalook photo.

Eventually, when nothing comes to mind, I reach for my phone and stare at the photo of the two of them. I trace my finger around the edges of their faces as though I might feel that level of desire. And for the first time in a long time, I think I do.

I feel it on the nights I sit next to Grant Dunn in his car. I feel it as I watch his hands on the wheel, and I feel it when he says my name. At some point I drift off. Thoughts of the Dunns fill my dreams.

I wake abruptly with a dry mouth and a stiff neck. It's still dark out. In my dream, I was at a party with Grant. Josie had followed us there, and no matter how many times we told her to go, she stayed. I don't recall what occurred after that—I only know I awoke to the sound of a scream lodged deep in my throat.

~

THREE NIGHTS LATER, I'M WALKING HOME. I'M NOT WALKING because I've missed the bus. I'm walking to punish myself. I swore I wouldn't get on Instalook, and I've been on Josie's page fifty-two times today. After the nineteenth time, I made myself start marking it down just so I know how severe the punishment needs to be. At this point, I'll be walking home all week.

The problem is, the reason I can't stop, is Josie hasn't posted, and it's killing me. The holidays are coming, and this time of the year is the worst. The days are shorter, and the nights are endless. Needless to say, I'm about as low as one can get and desperate for a plan— something, anything— to ease the loneliness of going home to an empty apartment.

Also, three days is an eternity. I think of all the reasons she wouldn't have posted. Maybe she's sick. Maybe Grant has died. Maybe she has died. The latter wouldn't be as bad as the former. But still.

More likely though, it's something slightly more plausible... like she's busy or her phone broke.

I've considered all the ways I could go about finding out how to fix this. I've run through all the ways I can insert myself into their life. I need answers. I need more. I did a search to find their address. It wasn't hard to find them.

Trouble is, I don't have a working car, so I can't drive by. I consider Ubering it or calling a cab, but those things leave records. And I know better.

But all bets are off if there's nothing on Instalook by tomorrow. Then maybe I'll ask Tyler if I can borrow his.

I pull my coat tighter around me, and I pick up my pace. It's colder out than I thought. I consider scheduling an appointment for a nose job or breast implants—something just to see his face again. Of course, there is the issue with how I'll pay for it all. Maybe I'll use Stacey's social and open one of those medical credit accounts. Or maybe Grant will stop with the ghosting he's doing, or maybe his wife will post to Instalook and then I won't have to do any of that.

In the meantime, I walk on into the night. Obviously, I'm secretly hoping Grant will drive by and offer me a ride, and I figure walking is my silent call. As luck would have it, it works. I almost can't believe it when I spot the familiar headlights. It's astounding how one can go from such a low to such a high in a matter of seconds. Astounding.

He doesn't ask me to get in this time. I just do.

"Jesus. Izzy. Why are you walking on a night like this?" He turns up the heat. "Do you not have any family?"

I shake my head and wonder why he's asking such obvious questions. His expression is fixed, and his tone isn't soft and smooth. It's hurried.

"Things have been hectic," he says with a heavy sigh. He leaves it at that. I do, too.

I'm sad when we pull up to the apartment complex that isn't mine.

"Thank you for the ride."

He rests his hand on my knee. Briefly. "Anytime."

I reach for the door handle. The door is locked, so I look over at him. "Why didn't you text tonight?"

I shrug.

He purses his lips and sadness sweeps across his face. "I was hoping you would..."

Suddenly, I'm screaming on the inside. I could burst with happiness. It's dark outside but I swear I see all the colors of the rainbow. I press my lips to one another. "I didn't want to bother you."

"Are you kidding?" he says. "This time with you, this is one of the highlights of my day."

"Thank you," I reply, and then hurriedly and stupidly, I add, "Me, too."

I exit his car, and that's when I see we have a problem. Tyler is standing at the bottom of my stairs. He's watching me, and when our eyes meet, he comes jogging across the street.

"What are you doing?" I seethe.

He slings his arm around my neck. "Looking for you," he tells me. I smell the pot on his breath.

I tell him I'm tired, which I am. Trouble is, I can't very well walk to my apartment with Grant watching. So, I stand there making small talk until eventually Grant drives away.

Exactly three minutes later my phone chimes. *Friend of yours?*

Something like that. I text back.

Just making sure, he writes and then radio silence.

I don't hear from Grant Dunn again for six days.

I shouldn't have been so stupid. I contemplate all possible scenarios where I went wrong. He probably realized I stalk his wife online. He isn't stupid. He makes a living fixing people's flaws. I shouldn't have said 'me too.' I should have told him how I really feel. I should have been more imaginative. It didn't even make sense in the context of things. Now he thinks not only am I illiterate but I have a thing for losers, as well.

For six days I scan Josie's page. Thankfully, this time she posts updates. He buys her a new book, and flowers, lots of flowers. He brings her breakfast in bed. She posts about spin class and book club and brunch with her friends. That's the kind of woman who deserves a man like Grant Dunn. Not a girl who can't speak, not someone who has sex with men she doesn't even like. Not someone like me. I want to change this, but where do I begin? And then it hits me. I've taken my eye off what really matters. Her.

CHAPTER SEVENTEEN

JOSIE

I'm in the bath when Grant comes storming in. "I found these in your purse," he says, holding up the bottle of pills. His expression is pained.

"Beth thinks I need them."

"I know," he tells me. "But they're all accounted for. You haven't touched them."

"I'm not depressed, Grant." I sink lower into the water. "We've discussed this."

"I thought you said you'd try, though. I thought you were going to give this," he says rattling the bottle, "a shot."

"That was before," I say, and he knows which before I'm referring to. Before the dining room incident. "I changed my mind."

He doesn't say anything in return. He doesn't like to be reminded of his bad deeds. Not after he's worked so hard to make them right. I'm still angry with him, and he knows it.

"How many times do I have to say I'm sorry?" he asks as he climbs in with me. I scoot to make room, and it's so comfortable, this dance we do. Even though I want to be angry, and I am, I also want things to be normal again. There's relief in normalcy. I don't want to forgive him for what he's done. But I also don't want to walk on eggshells around him, either. I want a peaceful home for our children.

"It's healing nicely," he says, touching the torn skin on my back he has glued together.

"Yes," I agree. "Thankfully, it's only a surface wound."

"Superficial," he murmurs scratching the skin around it. It feels nice to have him touch me. Also, it itches like crazy as it heals.

"I don't want to fight," I tell him, peering up, my head on his chest. "The kids already sense something is wrong, and they have so much going on, us not speaking to one another, or worse, is the last thing they need."

He frowns. "I don't either."

I sigh heavily. "I also don't want to take antidepressants. I'm not depressed."

He pats my back. "I know. You just need a break."

"We both need a break."

"Speaking of which," he grins widely, "I've booked us a trip."

I cock my head. "When?"

"When we get out."

"What?"

"We're taking a long weekend."

"Where are we going?"

"That part," he says, "is a surprise."

"What about the kids?"

"They're staying with Beth's family."

"They hate the Joneses."

"They'll manage," he says convincingly. "It's only three days."

"But—"

"Josie—stop. I've packed you a bag. It's done," he pulls me closer. "Now, just enjoy it."

THE FLIGHT ATTENDANT BRINGS TWO CHAMPAGNE FLUTES. I TAKE A

photo and post it to Instalook with the hashtags #surprisetrip #wherearewegoing #besthusbandever #blessedlife

I feel guilty for leaving the kids with the Joneses. They're hardcore about daily prayer and ritual, and more than anything, I'm afraid that one or both of them will slip up. We're not nearly as disciplined in our home—not that the Jones's know that. But I guess they will now.

Grant pulls something from his carry-on. I'm checking the number of likes on my Instalook post when he slips something into my lap. I look down. A little blue box rests on my thighs. "For you," he says. "I want this trip to set things right between us."

My eyes light up. "I want that too," I tell him, lifting the lid from the box.

I gasp when I see the diamond bracelet. It's gorgeous. A woman from across the aisle stares. The flight attendant asks if she can take a peek. She asks if we'd like her to take a photo to mark the occasion. She thinks it's our anniversary. "How many years now?" she asks.

"Eighteen," I tell her.

"Well," she smiles. "Aren't you lucky?"

"I'm the lucky one," Grant pipes in. I can see by the way she looks at him she's enamored by his charm. His money doesn't hurt. But his looks kill.

She snaps the photo, and I post it to Instalook. Caption: And there's more. #hejustgetsbetter #blueboxlove

Grant places his hand on my thigh. "So you like it then?"

"I love it," I promise. I lean over and kiss his cheek.

"Good," he quips. "Now, I need to focus." I look on as he pulls a book from his bag and opens it. I pull up Instalook. "Oh—" he says, pulling another book from his bag. This one I'd recognize anywhere. It's my Bible. "Beth suggested you study Proverbs. I have several passages bookmarked."

I put my phone away. We don't speak for the rest of the flight.

LATER, AFTER WE'RE CHECKED INTO OUR HOTEL, AND I'VE SNAPPED A few photos of the view from our balcony for Instalook, with the hashtag #scottsdaleitis, Grant takes my hand and leads me to the bed. I go willingly, because I can't take one more minute of silence nor of staring at words I can't find meaning in.

Ever since we've landed, he's taken work call after work call. Something has blown up, and I can see that it has him on edge. I try to be understanding. When he steps out to take another call, I check on the kids. They don't seem as annoyed as I'd figured they'd be.

After I end the call, I unpack both our suitcases. By the time I finish, and he still isn't back, I check Instalook. I converse with fans for a bit about sights we should check out while in the area, and then I resume half-immersing myself in my required reading material. I don't yet understand what I'm supposed to be looking for in the text, but I know it's just a matter of time before it becomes apparent. I'm just about to give up when he comes back.

"Sorry," he says. "This is what I get for trying to get away."

"Is everything okay?" I ask, motioning toward the phone. The calls, the intrusion into our lives, it isn't abnormal. I'm trying to be kind.

"Just work stuff," he says. "I want to lie with you before I have to hop on another call."

"All right." I place my hands on my hips. He's already halfway to the bed. Sex will resolve some of the tension. I watch as he strips out of his clothes. I start to remove my own when he holds his hand up. "Come here," he says, and I do. My husband desires obedience. There's security in that.

He takes me in his arms, and I feel that something in me, the weight of the day, the weight of the past few weeks, slowly melts away. He sits back on the bed and I sit facing him. I start to unbutton my blouse when he stops me. "Would you mind?" he asks nodding. "It's been a long day," he sighs. "And I could really use some relief."

My eyes widen. I'd like to say I'm not surprised, but that would be a lie.

"Josie," he says, getting my attention. I feel tears coming. Grant thinks crying is a form of manipulation. "Come on," he says almost earnestly. "Don't leave me hanging."

I scoot lower on the bed, and I give him what he wants. This is the thing no one tells you about loving a person, I think, working him the way I know he likes. They're bound to hurt you at some point. You can't make a lifelong commitment to another person and come out unscathed. No one does. You just do the best you can to minimize the damage.

〜

"WE NEED TO TALK," GRANT TELLS ME, WAKING ME FROM SLEEP. I glance toward the balcony. It's dark out. I have no idea what time it is, or how long I've been asleep. He brushes the hair from my face. Drool has matted it to my cheek. My mouth is dry. "I have something for you."

He's holding a small box. I blink as he kneels before me. He thrusts the box in my direction. I'm not fully awake.

"You didn't have to do this," I tell him.

"I wanted to."

I eye the box. He holds it up to me, and when I reach for it he pulls it away. "First, there's something I need to know..."

"Okay," I answer unsure where this is going.

He studies my face carefully. "If you could do it all over again...would you?"

"Do what?"

He frowns. "This. Us."

I narrow my gaze. "Of course, why?"

He lets out a long heavy sigh. "It's nothing," he says. He looks

131

relieved, and this is the man I know. He doesn't ask questions like this. "Just something I needed to hear."

"Here," he says, thrusting the box at me. "Open it."

I lift the lid and inside are the most gorgeous emerald earrings I've ever seen. They're drop earrings surrounded by the tiniest understated diamonds that make the rest of it just pop. "Thank you," I say, my face flush. "This is too much."

"There's more…" He tells me, and he stands and walks over to the closet and opens it. "They will go perfectly with the dress I purchased."

"Grant… wow. I don't know what to say."

He smiles. "You've said enough."

He helps me slip into the gown, and then we're off into the night, no worse for the wear.

Dinner turns out to be lovely. We don't talk about forced feedings or New Hope or even the kids. We don't speak much at all, in fact. In the end, I know how it'll turn out. He'll strip me out of this expensive dress, and make love to me with the earrings on. Later when I go to the sink to clean up and wash my face, I'll remove them. I'll carefully lay them next to the others, a long line of gifts that remind me all things broken can be fixed. A beautiful reminder of remorse. I'll snap a photo of them next to my dress on the hanger and post it to Instalook with the caption: *he loves me.*

CHAPTER EIGHTEEN

IZZY

Serendipity, it turned out to be. I first saw it in Josie's photo sitting on Grant's bedside table. These are the things one can come to know about a person by studying their behavior online. Innocent things. Intimate things. Things one can use to their advantage. Things like books. People like people who have the same tastes. It offers a sense of validation. Most people need that. Even the Grant Dunns of the world aren't immune to neediness in that sense. The only difference is he doesn't want you to know he has insecurities, whereas most people shout them from the rooftops. I once read a study about the negative to positive ratio in regard to the kinds of things people say online. Also, how much is fact and how much is fiction. It was enlightening. It's strange what people connect to.

"I can't believe you're reading that," he says. He looks over at me, devilish grin and all. "I thought no one read Dickens anymore." I smirk. It's been days since I've seen that grin. Maybe Josh was right when he said fire needs air to breathe.

"What if I didn't take you home immediately?" he quips. "What if we went for a little drive instead?"

I glance down at my hands. Anything to avoid appearing too eager. People like it when you're unsure. It gives them the satisfaction of convincing you. People like to win. Especially people like Grant Dunn.

"We can discuss the book," he adds.

I pretend to think it over. My eyes dart to the clock on the dash. This buys me time. He wants to have to work for it.

I watch as his fingers tighten around the wheel. He doesn't know it, but he appreciates the suspense. It's the best part of the game. *Will she or won't she?*

Finally, I shrug as though to say *why not.* He flips the blinker and pulls onto the highway. It's a good thing I am prepared. I did actually read some of that stupid book. Not enough to really discuss it in detail. But enough so he won't know the difference. Mostly though, he'll want to tell me his interpretation rather than hear mine. He'll be nice and satisfied if I throw in a question, just a slight *but what if.* He'll want a minuscule difference of opinion, a slight disagreement. But not a real one. He'll correct me and feel smart doing so. With a bit of hesitation, I'll agree, before I finally admit the truth—that I have no idea how I could have missed that.

~

WE DRIVE INTO THE NIGHT. HE PUTS THE TOP DOWN. IT'S CHILLY out, but I don't care. This feels dangerous, reckless—necessary ingredients. He turns up the heat, and then grabs his coat from the back. He lays it over me. Holiday lights twinkle in the distance. "Won't you be cold?" I ask, but it's so loud in a convertible. I hadn't realized it would be this loud. I'm not sure whether he hears me or not.

He smiles. "I spend my days in a hospital, remember? The OR trains you to embrace the cold."

I hadn't thought of it that way. But that's the thing about Grant

Dunn: He's considerate. He takes thought a level or two above what you'd expect. He's unpredictable.

Eventually, we pull off the highway, and the lights fade until it is just us on a two-lane open road.

"Do you like to go fast?" he asks, a wry grin plastered on his face like it's a permanent fixture. Like it comes with the car.

I want to say yes. But I jut out my bottom lip and raise my brow instead, because it's hard to answer that question when you don't even own a vehicle.

"Would you like to find out?"

"Sure," I yell. I don't mean to. I'm just not sure how my voice is going to come out in the open air.

He floors it, which forces my head back against the seat. It's like being in a slingshot, being launched into outer space. It feels so good, so free. I would go to the edges of space with Grant Dunn. I would go anywhere with him.

We drive for a bit, fast, too fast. Eventually, he slows and pulls off onto the side of the road. He puts the car in park, and I should be scared about what comes next, about being out in the middle of nowhere with a man I hardly know. But I'm not. I smooth my hair away from my face.

It's dark, practically pitch black, save for the headlights. "Look up," he says, and I do. There are stars up above, entire galaxies I've never seen.

We sit there in silence for a long while. I inhale the fresh air, fill my lungs with it. I hold it in. I never want to let go. It smells like pine needles and freedom. I'd stay here forever staring at this kind of magic if I could.

But everything changes.

At some point he gets out of the car, walks around to my side and opens the door. "It looks better from the hood," he motions. He offers his hand. "That and it's warmer there."

"There," he says, and I perch myself on the hood. He stands in front of me. Neither of us are looking at the stars anymore.

135

"Mr. Dunn—" I say, knowing what's coming. Part of me is trying to put the brakes on. Part of me can't help myself.

He shakes his head slowly. "Don't call me that. Call me Grant," he tells me. "Or doctor, if you must," he adds with a sly smile. It fades quickly. Too quickly. "Anything but that."

It feels awkward with him standing over me. I want him to make his move, and yet I don't, because I know this is the start of something. Also, that it's the beginning of the end.

"Okay," I say. "Thank you, Grant."

"Better."

I rest on my elbow and let my head fall all the way back until it feels like I'm looking at the whole world upside down. This is the way I feel. Upside down. Inside out. A thousand tiny instances I could have stopped this one-way train we're on, and in all of them I could never quite make myself pull the cord. I know it only goes one way or the other from here, and I know that if I reject him which way that is. The rides will stop, this— whatever this is— it all goes away. And to be frank, I'm sick of things going away.

I don't know what to say in that moment, so I default to sarcasm. "You could kill me out here and no one would know…"

He lowers his voice, and I don't know how he does it but it's so thick and smooth it's suffocating. "I'd never hurt you Izzy," he says, and it's the first time I know for sure he's telling me a lie.

"Oh, I don't know about that."

He leans down, and he's so close now I can taste my future. All I know is I want him in it.

I raise my head, meeting him in the middle. My world is right side up again. He kisses me, sucking my bottom lip between his teeth. He's not hesitant, but he's not rushed, either. He's the perfect mixture of everything.

He pulls away, and he searches my eyes. Carefully. Thoroughly. It's just me and him, galaxies and the headlights.

After several moments, he moves away, and I think maybe he's lost his nerve. *Yes, I want to tell him. You will be giving up a lot. There's no going back. Trust me, I know.*

He takes my hand and pulls me into a standing position. Then he takes the coat he's slung over my shoulders and lays it on the hood. He nods, and I realize he hasn't lost his nerve. He's setting the stage. "Is this all right with you?"

This is my chance. One way or the other, I have a decision to make. *It's already been made. It was made when you got in the car. It was made when you pulled off the highway. It was made the first time you saw his stupid face.* I look up at the stars, and then I meet his gaze directly. "Yes. This is perfect."

He peels me out of my jeans. The cold hits me hard. All I feel is his warmth. A part of me cringes. Usually, I like to prepare myself for moments like this. I'm sure I smell like work, but he doesn't seem to care. "I'd like to take my time with you, Izzy; I'd like to show you what I'm capable of," he whispers. "But we haven't got time for that."

I nod as though I know what he means. I've got all the time in the world.

He lays me back on the hood and parts my knees. I listen as he tears the condom wrapper, and I'm grateful one of us has thought ahead. Suddenly, I feel him warm and rigid against my thigh. It causes me to jump. He places his palms on either side of me, lowers down. His lips meet my neck, grazing the spot just behind my ear. "You'll have to forgive me," he says. "I hate condoms. But I don't trust that friend of yours."

My eyes widen. It's such a strange thing to say when you're about to make love to someone for the first time. I hadn't considered that this might not be love.

"I have wanted this for so long," he says, kissing me on the mouth. "So long."

"Me too," I assure him.

He slides into me slowly, gently, carefully, and he moves with precision. "I want you to tell me what you like," he says searching my eyes. "I want this to last."

"This," I murmur breathlessly. "I like this."

"Yes," he tells me. "But what do you want?"

"I want you to fuck me," I say, and so he does.

I look up at the stars as he moves into me, and I'd like to say I'm thinking what a mistake this all is. I know I should care about his wife. But the truth is Josie Dunn never crosses my mind.

CHAPTER NINETEEN

JOSIE

I don't have time for this. Not today. I have a to-do list a mile long, and I was hoping for an afternoon to myself just to catch my breath.

"Avery, please. Calm down," I say into the phone.

"I CAN'T CALM DOWN," she yells, causing me to pull my ear away from the speaker. I can't make out the rest of what she's saying. I put the phone to my ear again, but this time all I hear is her heavy breathing, snot and tears. Finally, there's a break. "Did you hear me at all? I NEED YOU TO COME AND GET ME."

"Avery—"

"They cut me from the dance team."

Great. I throw up my hands. "Why would they do that?"

She sniffles, blows her nose, into her collar no doubt. Then she starts crying again. "I don't know."

"Well, what did they say?" I shouldn't sound so annoyed, but I can't help myself. There's a limit one can take where teenage dramatics are concerned. I search for my keys.

"It's a long story," she tells me, her tone matching my level of irritation. "Can you come and get me or not?"

When I don't answer immediately—I'm still searching for the

keys and wondering where I could have placed them—she lets out a long sigh. "Or should I just call Beth?"

"Beth? Why would you say that?" I reach into the drawer and grab the spare set of keys.

"She told me to call if I ever needed anything."

I roll my eyes. "I'll be there in ten minutes. Wait for me on the bench out front."

"Fine," she says. Not *thank you*. Just fine. For a moment I consider teaching her a lesson for talking to me this way. I consider letting her ride it out. But then she probably would call Beth, and I'd have to explain and it's just not worth it. There are easier ways to teach lessons. Also, I can't recall a time when I've heard her this distraught, and she hasn't so much as gotten a bad note home before, so getting cut from anything, much less dance, doesn't seem like her. Dance is her life. They say you're supposed to watch out for these things with teenagers. Especially in a competitive environment like this. Private school, especially one filled with New Hope members, is no joke. Look for changes in attitudes, quitting or ceasing the things they love, they warn. It can be more than just a sign of growing up. It can lead to trouble. To darker things, things I don't want to think about. They tell you all the signs to look for. They just never tell you what to do when you come face to face with them.

WHEN I ARRIVE AT THE SCHOOL, AVERY ISN'T WAITING ON THE bench. I text her, and she replies immediately. She's waiting in the assistant principal's office. He would like to speak with me.

I don't know if it's just my imagination, or if everyone really is glaring at me as I make my way down the hall to his office. When I reach the door, I see Mr. Hines through the small glass window. He's sitting at his desk, hands folded, facing the door. He doesn't immediately see me. Avery is seated across from him. He's speaking to her. His face is set, stern. I know that look well. She nods, but I can't see her face. She buries it in her hands. Her shoulders heave. She's sobbing. My heart leaps into my throat; I hadn't been prepared for this. My hand grips the doorknob. Instinctively, I want to kill him for making my daughter feel this way. Something innate comes to the surface, and I'm ready to pounce. I twist the knob. "What is—" One look at Avery, her mascara running down her face, her eyelids swollen, nostrils raw, and the rest of my sentence lodges in my throat. It's probably a good thing, as I realize that anything I say is going to be the wrong thing.

"Please, Mrs. Dunn—" He cuts me off and motions to a chair beside my daughter. "Have a seat." He speaks calmly. Authoritatively. Like my husband. I wonder if there's a class they give on this kind of stuff. *How to get women to do what you want.*

I want to dig my heels in, to grab my daughter and get the hell out of there. Somehow, I see the end result, and I stop myself. I'd never hear the end of it if she were kicked out of school. There are things I've been warned about, but sometimes you can't learn until you suffer the consequences.

Still, I look down at Avery, and I do as he asks.

She looks over at me and wipes her eyes with the back of her hand. "I didn't do it, Mom," she cries. She speaks between sobs, furiously. This is not the Avery I know. "I promise. It wasn't me," she says, and a thought crosses my mind. I push it away. *How well can we ever really know our children?*

"Mrs. Dunn, I called you in to talk about an incident—" he starts. I place my hand on Avery's knee, and he pauses. He peers at me over the rim of his glasses. It feels very official. He wants to see that I understand as much. I do. If you try to boil the entire ocean at once it doesn't work. "A very serious incident."

I lift my brow.

He shifts his gaze to my daughter and then looks back at me. "I don't presume you're aware of the situation."

"I'm aware that Avery was cut from the dance team."

He seems confused. "Avery is being accused of harassing a fellow classmate."

I glance over at my daughter. She's staring at me, wide-eyed. I know this expression. But I don't know what to make of it. "Harassing? Harassing who?"

"One of our students has been hospitalized after an attempted suicide. When her mother checked her phone, she found dozens of messages from your daughter. Threatening messages."

My mouth hangs open. A saying comes to mind: Those who are shocked should be shocked more often.

"Mom—I swear. I never sent Laura Duffy anything. I swear."

I shift in my seat. I open my mouth to speak before closing it again.

"I swear," Avery says. "I hardly even talk to Laura Duffy."

"How do we know it was my daughter sending the messages?"

He slides a stack of papers toward me. It appears he was expecting the question. I glance down at the text exchanges, most of them with my daughter's profile picture next to them. "They were sent from her Instalook account."

I glance up and meet his eye before looking over at my daughter.

"BUT IT WASN'T ME!" Avery begins to lose it. It takes a lot, but there's a little of her father in her, nonetheless.

"Can we prove they came from her?" I study my daughter carefully.

"We're currently looking into that. Investigators have spoken with Avery and are in the process of gathering information."

I meet his gaze, letting my tight smile convey the simmering fury. "Wait—you let cops speak to my daughter without my knowledge or permission?"

"Mrs. Dunn—"

"Don't—" I say. I stand to leave and pat Avery's shoulder, ushering her to follow suit.

Mr. Hines is the last to stand. He clears his throat. "In light of how serious these allegations are, I'm afraid we have to suspend Avery until further notice."

"You can't even prove she's done anything."

"No—" he says. "But we have to keep the campus safe and secure in the meantime."

~

LATER IN THE CAR I TURN TO AVERY. HER NOSE IS BURIED DEEP IN her cell phone, her fingers working furiously. "Just tell me what happened," I say.

She stops texting and blows her nose into the bottom of her shirt. Finally, she sighs. "My life is over. That's what happened."

"Your life is not over, Avery."

"It is over! You heard him. I'm expelled. Daddy is going to kill me."

"You father is not going to kill you." *Me, now that's another story.*

She turns back to her phone. Explaining the situation to her friends seems more pressing.

"Please," I say, reaching for the phone. "Just tell me what the hell is going on."

She throws up her hands dramatically and I understand that to her it does feel like her life is over. "Someone is framing me," she tells me. Then she shrugs as though it is the most logical and likely thing in the world.

"And why would someone do that?"

"I don't know. Because they can."

I purse my lips. When she was little, I knew how to fix things. Or at least where to start or what to try. They grow up, but nothing really changes. It's always going to be a guessing game. "I have to ask—did you send those texts to Laura Duffy? Because if you did Avery—they will find out."

"But I didn't," she scoffs. "I told you that. They can't just accuse

143

me of something I didn't do. I know my rights!" she exclaims wildly, with all the false bravado a teenage girl can muster.

"You see, Avery—they can, and they have."

She glares at me her mouth agape. "WOW. My own mother doesn't even believe me. What happened to being innocent until proven guilty?"

"Avery. Honey," I say softening my tone. I reach over and place my hand on hers. She pulls away. "It isn't that I don't believe you. That's not what I said." I take a deep breath in and slowly let it out. "I've never known you to do anything like this. Ever."

She looks up at me, and I see something in her expression flicker. Relief, maybe.

I tilt my head and narrow my gaze. "It's just that we have to prove your innocence, which means I am going to need you to be straightforward with me. About everything."

"I am."

We sit in silence for a long time before she speaks again.

"You know what this means?" she asks without waiting for a reply. "I have to miss Christmas competition. I'm not allowed to go to the formal, and I'm cut from all pep rallies. I'll miss finals. They can flunk me."

I sigh, and she begins crying again.

"We'll fix this before that happens," I promise.

"There's no point."

"Are you sure you have no idea who sent those texts? You can tell me Avery. You can tell me anything."

She shifts in her seat and glares at me. "Of course, I don't know. LIKE I TOLD YOU A THOUSAND TIMES." she screams. "I should have known you wouldn't believe me."

"It's not that I don't believe you. I just have to know where to go from here," I tell her thinking of her father.

"You know what? Just forget it," she says. I watch as she folds her arms and shifts away from me. "I don't care if I ever go back to that place."

"You're going back to school, Avery."

When she starts crying again, I impulsively pull into Lucky's parking lot. I need something—coffee, green tea, anything to get me through the rest of the afternoon. No sandwiches this time. I couldn't stomach one even if I wanted to.

I park and order Avery to come in with me. When she refuses, I take the phone from her hand. "This is non-negotiable."

The normal barista is working the counter. The one from the park. The weird one. The one I invited to church. The one who made me promise to keep her secrets. It seems like such an odd thing to say now. She doesn't notice me standing there. Not at first. She's busy staring at her phone. When I get up to the counter she looks up. Her eyes grow wide. Her knuckles whiten around the phone.

"You," she says, and I can't read her expression, but it's almost like I've caught her doing something she shouldn't be. Texting on the job?

"Don't worry," I say, nodding. "I won't tell."

She sort of smiles and takes my order. I realize I shouldn't have come. Being here reminds me of the sandwich incident and my reconciliation with Grant feels too fragile just yet for any reminders. "The cappuccino is for my daughter," I say, glancing back at Avery, who is sulking in a chair. She too is staring at her phone. I remember all the times I'd take her after school for donuts or hot chocolate or a croissant when she was little. Looking back, those seem like such innocent times. Before all the rules. Before I really minded having to follow them. I thought life was hectic then. I thought they'd keep me—keep us— safe. I had no idea.

Back then, I had no context of what parenting an adolescent would bring. I only knew what it had been like when I was a teenager, and still, that was seeing it from the other side. To be a parent, in charge of so many emotions while trying to manage your own, is something else entirely. "She was cut from drill team today," I mention. I leave out the part where she was expelled from school entirely. Sometimes the truth is too much.

She glances at Avery. "I'll add extra whip."

"Thanks," I say. "But I don't think that cheers teenage girls up these days...I haven't a clue what does, actually...maybe nothing." I speak nervously. Off the cuff, which isn't like me.

"How's she taking it?"

"I'm not sure yet," I say. I don't say that she doesn't talk to me anymore, not about dance, not about most things. She has her friends for that, and with the invention of smartphones those friends are ever present in our lives. I don't say this, but it makes me long for the days I just wanted a break, even five minutes to go to the bathroom alone. In those days, at least I knew what was troubling my daughter, and I knew how to fix it.

I notice a bouquet on the counter. I lean down to inhale their scent. It helps hold back the tears that threaten my eyelids.

She smiles.

I inhale deeply. I probably look like a fool. But I'm an expert at keeping my emotions at bay. "Lilies. They're my favorite."

She nods. "Mine, too," she tells me solemnly. I see sadness in her eyes. She hands me my green tea. Her hand touches mine. I glance over my shoulder at Avery. When I look back at the girl, she's crying. "Are you okay?'

I hand her a napkin. "It's my anniversary."

"Oh," I say. "Well—"

"He's dead."

A lump forms in my throat. "I'm sorry."

"He always sent lilies."

"It's fine," she says. I stare at the floor as she rings me up. Avery sidles up to me and takes her coffee.

"Have you given my invitation any thought?" I tread carefully. Now that things are better between Grant and I, and Beth too, I regret asking.

"I don't know..."

"That's okay," I say. "It's probably not your thing anyway."

"Say," she says, her tone serious. Intense. "I could work with your daughter. I used to teach dance. Ballet mainly. But I'm familiar with all kinds. My mother owned a studio. I mean, that was a long time ago—but still."

"Wow," I say, caught off-guard by her offer. "That's very kind of you. But—"

"Wait," Avery says, interrupting me. Her face is lit up. "A private tutor. That's exactly what I need. I've been asking..."

"I'm really cheap," the girl smiles. "As in free of charge."

"That's not necessary—"

She furrows her brow. "The truth is, I just really miss dance."

"This is perfect," Avery claps. "This way I won't miss out. If I keep up my skills—if I get better—maybe they'll still let me compete. "

I look from Avery to the barista. She looks so happy. A complete one-eighty from just a few minutes ago in the car. I shrug. "Guess I'll need your contact info."

CHAPTER TWENTY

IZZY

I know I shouldn't have done it. But I couldn't help myself. I hadn't seen Grant Dunn in five days. We had sex on the hood of his car, and then he ghosted me. To his credit, he did throw in a dozen flowers first. Her favorite, as it turns out.

I'll admit. I was drunk and a little high too when I stumbled on Avery Dunn's Instalook page. And the more I drank and the more I looked at her spoiled little life, the more I realized why her father hadn't called. He was too busy making her life perfect. He shouldn't have to work so hard to give her all that. She should be happy just to have a dad like him. But she isn't. It's obvious. Also, I recognized her face as one of the kids who "studies" at Lucky's. She's not one of the troublemakers. But she doesn't exactly clean up after herself, either. Why would she with a life like that?

So, I did it. I found one of her friends, and I started dripping DMs. Just one or two, here and there. But over those five days, the less I heard from Grant Dunn the more I sent.

But the invitation to teach her to dance...well, that was luck. I didn't know my messages would get her kicked off the dance team. But I'm not the least bit sorry, either.

"I THINK WE SHOULD GO AWAY TOGETHER," GRANT TELLS ME IN THE office at Lucky's. We've just finished having sex, our third time. It's after closing, and Stacey's desk seemed more appealing than Grant's car. This time was better than last time, but not as good as the first. Maybe it never gets to be as good as it was the first time again. I remember that with Josh. Maybe it's a high you chase forever. I'm willing.

"Where would we go?" I ask with a smile. This is the best suggestion I've heard all week. I can't take my eyes off him. Mostly, I'm just so relieved he finally called.

He raises his brow, and clearly he has secrets I'd be privileged to know. "You leave that to me."

I button my shirt and then hand him his tie.

"But Izzy," he says. His monotone voice comes out rough. "There's something on my mind. Something serious."

I cock my head.

There's not an ounce of hesitation in him. Grant Dunn is not the kind of man who skirts around issues. I could get used to this. I've been waiting all my life. "I'd like to know why you haven't invited me back to your place?"

My cheeks grow hot. I don't have an answer at the ready. *I am not good enough for you.* "I-I—"

"Stop." He cuts me off as he clasps his belt. "There's only one right answer here…"

I wait for it as he rubs his jaw.

"I have to know it's not because of that friend of yours."

He meets my eye then. "No," I say. "I just didn't think you wanted to see my apartment."

"What? Why?"

"I mean…there isn't much to see."

He shrugs, holds out his hands and looks around. "It has to be better than this."

I don't say anything. He has a point.

He walks over to where I'm standing, and he smiles intently. "I know," he utters. "I'm probably rushing things." He leans in and covers my mouth with his. I intertwine my hand in his hair, urging the back of his head closer. He pulls back. "But my God. I just can't get enough of you."

"I'm not seeing Tyler anymore," I offer, and then and there I know I'd promise anything he asked of me. He tastes that good on my lips.

His eyebrows raise and his hand flies to his chest. "Wow," he exhales. "I can't tell you what a relief that is. I know—I know," he adds, holding his palms toward me. "I'm not supposed to make demands. Especially given my own situation. But I can't help but want you all to myself. And I realized—what's so wrong with that?"

I feel butterflies in my stomach. "Nothing," I say, and I swear falling in love is the best thing ever. Grant Dunn is everything. There's only one small problem. He's married. Speaking of his wife, she's been quiet on Instalook lately. Grant hasn't mentioned it. He hasn't mentioned anything about his family, really. Mostly, he wants to know about me. Thankfully, I don't have to offer much. Typically, there isn't time for talking. I start to ask him about the flowers. I want to know why he didn't ask me about my favorite. But I'm probably overreacting. Also, it would seem kind of petty. Grant has never once given me the idea that he's the kind of man to take shortcuts.

Still, I couldn't sleep last night, thinking about it. So I studied his wife's latest Instalook posts. They've been a little vague lately.

But now, being here with him, I realize I'm probably making something out of nothing. It's like when you think about a red car and then before long red cars are all you see. I'm sure it's like that with the flowers.

"How about this—I'll pick you up Friday evening. Bring a packed bag to work with you."

"Sounds like you have it all figured out," I tell him, and there's a whisper—an inkling. It's nagging, eating at me. I realize I'll have to cancel my dance lesson with his daughter. This is better.

He winks. I can't help but wonder if he's done this before.

I slip my foot into my shoe. "What will you tell your wife?" I blurt out. I need to know. Instantly, I regret asking. His expression shifts, and I see something there I haven't seen before. There's a sense of protection in his eyes. She's off limits. That's what it says.

"As I said—you leave everything up to me," he tells me, and so I do.

HE'S WAITING FOR ME OUT FRONT FRIDAY NIGHT AS I LOCK UP.

"Ready?" he asks when I climb in the car. His expression is impassable.

I nod. A wide grin spreads across my face. I can't help it. My cheeks flush red. It's been forever since I've taken a weekend off. Sure, it will mean going several days without groceries, and probably only paying half the light bill this month, but it will be worth it. Once we're on the highway, I shift and lean over. I run my hand up Grant's thigh. He turns to look at me. "Someone's eager," he says.

"I haven't seen you since Wednesday."

"I know," he tells me, pursing his lips. "It's been a busy week."

"We could pull over."

"No." He looks over at me. "You'll learn to wait," he says, somewhat sternly. Then he smiles. "Trust me, it's better that way."

I think he's joking, although I'm not entirely sure. I decide to trust him.

"If you say so," I say finally. I'm a bit wounded. Sometimes you have to say what you mean and mean what you say. He's never rejected me before. I'm overreacting, I know. I'm showing my naiveté, my immaturity, by being upset over a little brush-off when he's carved out an entire weekend to be with me.

"This weekend is very important," he offers, as though he knows what I'm thinking. "There's a lot riding on it."

I tilt my head. He's right. "Like what?"

"Like whether or not we keep seeing each other."

"Oh," I say. Jesus. I hadn't expected that. My vision blurs.

"I realize you think I'm blunt. And you're right. But there's something you should know about me, Isobel. I have very peculiar tastes." His brow creeps toward his hairline. "I need someone I can trust."

"You don't think you can trust me?"

"I don't give my trust away blindly."

"Oh," I say. Grant Dunn seems to be incapable of lying. He doesn't soften the blow, that's for sure.

"I'm a very particular man, Izzy. It's like jumping from a building without a net, flying trapeze absent the harness, and if I can't trust you to take my life in your hands, then we can't be lovers."

My curiosity is piqued. "What sort of peculiarities?"

He smiles. "Oh, nothing too out there." He reaches over and pats my knee. "You'll see."

I chew at my bottom lip.

He moves his hand to mine, places it on top and gives it a tight squeeze. "I wouldn't want to spoil the fun."

WE ARRIVE AT THE CABIN CLOSE TO MIDNIGHT. IT'S REMOTE, BUT HE doesn't have trouble finding it so I presume he knows the place well. "Are we expecting others?" I ask, standing in the doorway. When we enter, I'm surprised to see the lights are on. A fire is already going.

"Nope," he exclaims. "Just the two of us."

I nod, breathe a sigh of relief. I look around the living area. It's a nice place. A little rustic, but charming.

"I have a guy who maintains the place. Brad. He makes sure things are kept neat and orderly," he tells me, his hands full of bags. He refuses to let me help. I study the outline of his shoulders as he sets them in the entry way. They're strong shoulders, wide. Large enough that you have to stretch yourself to wrap your arms around them. The kind Josh had. "I don't find arriving to a cold, dark cabin all that appealing. Do you?"

I shake my head. He hands me one of the bags. "The shower is straight through there," he points. "Put this on when you finish. I'll get our things settled."

The bathroom has been remodeled recently. It seems a bit newer than the rest of the place. I set the bag on the counter and carefully remove the items. There are only two: a white corset and panties. I hold them up and check myself in the mirror. Then I check the tag. He's gotten the size right. The tag says La Perla, and I can't imagine how much this cost. Or rather, I can, and it makes my heart race.

I shower, all the while thinking that I don't really know how to put a corset on. I know I won't look as good as Josie, or any of the women he sees on a daily basis for that matter. I consider how I might get out of it. He said there was a lot riding on this weekend, and I don't want my flaws to be one of them.

There's a soft knock at the door. "You need help in there?"

"No," I call out. My voice cracks. "I'm good."

I keep the water running; meanwhile I towel off and try to get a head start at making myself presentable. I shaved this morning, and sprung for a bikini wax yesterday (never again) but the cold has caused stubble to make a reappearance on my legs. I know Grant Dunn appreciates perfection. I decide to look it up and see if the internet could help me figure out the corset situation. Also, I need to have a look at Instalook. I need to know Josie's okay. Or at least find a reason not to feel bad about what I'm doing. Sometimes feelings sneak up on a person. But then I realize I left my phone on the bar. I make do with my imagination. When I've squeezed and shifted and arranged myself into Grant's gift, I glance up at myself in the mirror. I hardly recognize the reflection staring back at me. Running my fingers through my wet hair, I fan it out. Then I trace the smudged mascara under my eyes until it looks like someone else standing there. A better version of myself. It's really quite amazing what expensive underwear can do for a girl.

"Isobel," Grant calls. "Come on. I can't wait any longer..."

It sounds strange to hear someone call me a name that isn't mine. He never asked if Izzy was short for Isobel—he just assumed, and so I let him. Sometimes it's better that way.

"Coming," I say, and I take one last glance at myself. I think of Josie when I flip off the light switch. Has he brought her here? Surely. But she's never posted about it. That must mean it's sacred. Lucky me. When I exit the bathroom, Josie Dunn slips from my mind. The cabin is lit by dozens and dozens of candles.

"Wow," Grant says. He crosses the room in three strides. "You look even better than I imagined."

He's holding a glass of red, and I try to slide it from his hand.

"Uh-uh," he says. "None of this for you."

I furrow my brow.

He takes a sip and then sets the glass aside. "I'd like to talk first, and I can't have you falling asleep on me."

I smile. Wine does have that effect on me. I swear he thinks of everything.

"What are we discussing?" I ask, with the tilt of my head. I'm nervous, so I flirt. He remains serious.

"Our future."

I laugh, because I think he's kidding. "Aren't we getting a bit ahead of ourselves?"

"One can never be too prepared or think too far into the future, Isobel."

CHAPTER TWENTY-ONE

JOSIE

I wake up alone. It's always a bit disconcerting to reach over to Grant's side of the bed and find it empty. It's not that it's uncommon, given his profession, but a part of the agreement we have under the church's guidelines is that a wife is to wake before her husband. Thankfully, for me, I've always been an early riser. Still, it's a rule, and on the rare occasions I've broken it, it didn't go unnoticed.

In the haze of the space between consciousness and sleep, I remember that Grant is out of town. I relax into the bed. I haven't felt this rested in ages, I think, rubbing the sleep from my eyes. I prop myself up on my elbows and glance over at the clock on the wall. Whew. It's light out, but it's still early. I always loved the endless feel of Saturday mornings, when time is expansive, when the day is all stretched out before you as though it will never end.

Grant has gone up to the cabin to do some work on it and meet with contractors. The cabin is his passion project, and I won't lie, I was a bit relieved when he didn't ask me to go. After the week I've had, it's nice to have a weekend to myself.

Of course, that isn't the case this morning. I have a meeting with Mel. Tom's new wife seems to be acclimating well, or at least

Beth seems to think she is, but it's my duty to check up on her weekly, nonetheless.

I force myself out of bed pulling my robe tight. The house is quiet. James has gone to a debate team competition in Houston with the church. They like to show off the up and coming talent. But he seems to like it, and he's good, like his father, so I let it be.

Avery, I find, is still asleep. She's been sleeping a lot the past few days, so I was bummed when the girl from the coffee shop called and canceled today's dance lesson. No doubt, now she'll want me to take her shopping. Either that or schlep her friends around. Ironically, all I want to do is sleep.

MEL IS SPEAKING TO ME. I KNOW BECAUSE I CAN SEE HER MOUTH moving, but all I hear is ringing in my ears. She's holding the door in place, and she's waving me in. All the while, I just stand there, hands at my sides. Frozen. "Josie?"

I think she says my name once, twice, maybe three times. "Josie? Are you okay?"

I see her glance over her shoulder. My eyes follow hers. *No one is going to rescue you.*

My eyes shift as the dog comes barreling toward me. June loved that dog. I never did. I brace myself, knowing he'll dirty my slacks. They're new, and this outfit has gotten so many likes on Instalook that I can't bear to have him ruin them.

Thankfully, Mel catches him by the collar. I watch as she wrestles with the dog. It gives me an odd sense of satisfaction. Serves her right.

"You had me worried," she confesses, once things are under control—meaning, the housekeeper comes and takes possession of the dog. I don't recognize the lady. June never wanted any staff.

"I'm fine," I assure her. "I've always loved this house."

She ushers me through the doorway. Her expression is

relieved. She's transformed since the dinner party. "How lovely to see you."

"Likewise," I tell her. I'm struck by how much she looks like June. This makes the words difficult to get out. All I see is my friend. But I know that isn't possible. She's dead.

Mel shows me into June's sitting room. "Please, sit," she offers, fluffing her dress. She motions toward the table. There are biscuits and tea. The kind I used to tease June about. *You must have been a Brit in another life,* I'd tell her. Carbs are mostly forbidden on Beth's diet plan, but for the sake of politeness can sometimes be forgiven. "Tom tells me you like tea."

"Yes," I say to her, accepting the cup and saucer. June's china.

"So—how've you been?" I ask. I'm distracted, looking around, trying to mentally take inventory of what has changed and what hasn't. She's staring at me now, assessing me, her brow furrowed. I restate my question. "How are things?"

"Good," she says with a long sigh. She straightens her back. "Great—really."

I sip my tea.

She narrows her gaze. "Shouldn't we pray first?"

Of course. How could I have forgotten this? My first mistake. She's new. She's trying to make an impression. She'll want to do everything by the book.

I half-laugh and smooth my hair. "Oh, right," I tell her with a small wince. "I'm not used to leading. Forgive me."

She rubs her palms on her dress. She isn't sure what to say.

I hope this doesn't get back to Tom, because that means it will get back to Grant, and I can't have him thinking me incapable.

"Why don't I lead?" she says, finally.

I raise my brow. "That sounds perfect." I place my cup and saucer back in its rightful place on the coffee table. She waits as I fold my hands and bow my head. An *Austin Home and Garden* magazine catches my eye. I want to pick it up, but nothing interrupts prayer. I know the backyard on the cover well. It's Beth's.

But it's the address label that catches my eye. It's addressed to Mel, which seems odd given she hasn't lived here that long.

"Is something wrong?" she asks, shifting. I look up. "Would you prefer to lead?"

I inhale deeply, and then I stretch my arms out. I get my bearings. "No," I say, and one side of my mouth forms a smile. "It slipped my mind that Beth had the cover this month. I just realized I forgot to congratulate her."

She studies my shoes. Or the floor. It's hard to tell. I can see that she's taking my distraction personally. She has a right to. I hate being here, in June's house, with someone who isn't June. I hate that I'm wasting my Saturday having tea with someone I don't really care about. I don't care how she's getting on. Or explaining the rules. Or any of that. But I have to make myself. That's the deal I made.

She looks up and gives me a weak smile. The look robs me of my rage.

"I'm sorry," I offer. "I'm a bit distracted this morning. Teenagers. Can't live with 'em, can't live without them."

"So you don't mind if I lead us in prayer then?"

I almost do a double-take. I smile instead. "No, of course not. This is your home, so it only makes sense," I say, and the irritation resurfaces. It's not her home, it's June's, and aside from her being in it, nothing has changed.

She smooths her dress. I look on as she rubs her palms against her thighs. This is definitely getting back to my husband.

She's wearing a long floral dress, which is a bit different than June would've worn, a bit tighter. "That's a pretty dress," I say. I have to stop playing defense, stop making her work for small answers so that the conversation stays on the surface. That's not why I came.

"Thank you," she says, blushing, and I realize she's equally nervous.

We pray. Or rather she prays, and I listen. It goes on and on, and I'm impressed by her thoroughness. I remember a time I cared that much. Well, not quite *that* much. But surely, I cared.

"So tell me," I say when she's finished, and we've said our amens. "How do you like the neighborhood?"

"It's great—" she offers, fanning out the skirt of her dress once again. "I really have no complaints."

"And how are the children?" I ask. I can't help myself, I have to know. "Tom's children, I mean."

"Oh," she says, and she looks away briefly. I can see that she's taken aback. I don't think she expected me to pry. She smiles, but it doesn't reach her eyes. "They're fine."

"I figured," I tell her. "They're great kids."

"Well, yes. But they're hardly children anymore."

She's right. They can't be much younger than she is.

"Yes," I laugh. "I guess you don't realize other people's children grow up."

She presses her lips to one another and leaves it at that.

"And the Bible study?" I missed the last one, sadly. I skate just beneath the surface. "My daughter was cut from the dance team. It was a big deal."

She nods like she understands. She doesn't.

"How did you get on with the others?"

She lifts her cup from the table and sips her tea uncomfortably.

"That good?" I ask. Sometimes sarcasm works. Sometimes it doesn't.

"I'm not sure they like me," she replies earnestly, and in this case I made the right call. I can't help but get the feeling she thinks I'm one and the same.

"I'm sure you're wrong," I tell her, sipping my tea. "They can be a tough bunch to crack. But they mean well."

She leans in. "Can I ask you something?"

"Sure."

"Do you think they know about the baby?"

"The baby?" I say raising my brow. Something lodges in my throat. *Of course, the baby.* The flowy dress, the shotgun wedding, it all makes perfect sense now.

"No," I tell her. "I haven't heard anything." This latter is the truth. It's the best way to hide a lie.

She looks relieved. She visibly relaxes. I expect her to say more, but when she doesn't, I realize I'm going to have to ask. I cross and uncross my legs. Then I fold my hands and place them in my lap. "How far along are you?"

She looks away. "Not very far. It's just—we haven't told anyone…"

"How did you and Tom meet? I know you said on the street but—"

"Yes—about that," she says, cutting me off. "I figured you'd want to know."

"It's really not my business," I say. "You don't have to tell me if you don't want to." Another truth hidden in a lie.

She glances away, and her eyes fix on something. I follow her gaze to a photo of Tom and his kids. June isn't in the picture. "It wasn't easy," she says. "Being that Tom was married."

"I imagine not," I tell her. I see June's face where she does not. I remember when that photo was taken.

"I didn't mean to hurt anyone," she says, meeting my eye. "It was a hard decision, but in the end—" She pats her stomach. "I think the best one."

I don't respond. I look away, sip my tea, and stare at the floor.

"But there's something I have to know," she adds, which catches me off guard and causes me to look up. She isn't as green as she's led me to believe. I realize then why she's confiding in me—why she's so nervous. She needs an ally against the others. Tom is a leader within New Hope. Like my husband, and Beth's, he has a say in who comes and goes. They set the rules. The rest of us have to abide by them. But that doesn't mean we have to like it.

"I know I shouldn't want to know— but I do—from your perspective, were Tom and June happy?"

"Oh," I respond. Her question catches me by surprise. I take a deep breath in and settle myself. Hearing June's name on her lips feels like a bigger betrayal than I was prepared for. "I don't know. I mean, who's to say what happiness really is?"

"Yes," she answers. Her voice wavers. "But if you had to guess?"

I twist my lips. "No one really knows what goes on behind closed doors."

"That's true," she says. "But maybe if I had some sort of idea... maybe it would lessen the guilt."

$\sim$

"I FEEL GUILTY," I REMEMBER SAYING TO GRANT AT THE TIME. I CAN still picture the way we were back then, the two of us standing in our new home, waiting for the movers to arrive with our belongings. We were young and in love. And tired. Very tired. We didn't bring much. We didn't have to. The church leaders wanted us to have new furniture. It was a gift. To welcome us. Officially.

"There are other things to feel guilty about," he assures me. "New furniture is not one of them."

"I thought churches were supposed to be spiritual."

"What's not spiritual about receiving a gift?"

I cock my head, rub a chip in the paint on the wall. It makes it worse. Someday I'll learn. Not today. "It's the tithing I don't get."

"What's not to get?"

I shrug. "I just thought we were meant to collect money from those of us who have been blessed to give to the needy."

He pulls me in close and smiles. "No," he tells me shaking his head. "That's socialism."

I smile and rest my head against his chest. He always has a different way of looking at things.

"You want to talk about guilt —" he says, taking me by the

shoulders. He pulls me away so he can see my face. "I feel terrible about the decision they made. You shouldn't be made to do extra chores." He frowns. I see the remorse in his eyes. He looks away. "I give them enough money. There are other ways for them to get the point across."

I notice that he doesn't use the word punishment. That's what it was, really. Scrubbing floors. Cleaning toilets. All for ordering takeout. *Effort is everything. Intention is important.*

"It's okay. I survived."

"No," he says. "Maybe you're right." I see the light in his eyes shift. "Maybe we shouldn't accept their gift."

I laugh. "I've earned that furniture," I tell him, thinking of all the bathroom stalls I knelt in last week.

"Oh, Josie. I know. The guilt eats at me every day."

I do a double-take. "Why?"

"Because you've taken on all of this," he motions around the empty space. "And all I do is work. If I'm not at the hospital, I'm at the office. I go to sleep thinking about charts, and they're the first thing I see when I wake up."

"Yes," I say pulling him closer. "Your practice has grown significantly. Faster than you expected." He reminds me of this whenever a new rule is handed down. Last week, it was hospitality committee. Every wife must take part. The leadership team decided it was no longer optional. That's why I was punished. I'd been tasked with making a week's worth of meals for a family in need, even though we are in the middle of a move ourselves. And by family *in need,* New Hope has defined this as any couple new to the congregation. Problem was, they cut our gas, and my stove wasn't working. I ordered takeout delivery. It was apparently the wrong thing to do. Impersonal and tacky, Beth called it. I should have told her if I wasn't able to keep my commitment. *Communication is key.* I complained to Grant. I shouldn't have. He works so hard for us. I must never forget to be grateful. "But this is what we wanted."

He gives me the side-eye. "Is it though?"

~

I LIE THERE ON THE EDGES OF SLEEP, STARING AT THE CEILING. I'M counting the minutes I might get between now and James's next feeding. Grant refuses to let me bring him to bed. He wants me to let him cry it out. We argued about that again last night. He hasn't spoken to me since.

"I don't want you taking the baby around those people," he tells me in the darkness. I'm so thankful to finally hear his voice that I forget to be angry. Also, it takes me a moment to comprehend what he's said.

"What people?"

"Any of them. Anyone who isn't a part of the church. Anyone I can't be sure of."

"Grant—" I say. "They're my friends."

He rolls over. I stare at his back. It's familiar and foreign all at once. Maybe this is the way this is supposed to be. I wouldn't know. All I know is suddenly there's an invisible wall between us, and it's growing taller. It's become one I can't breach. "I don't care," he sighs. "He's my son."

I sit up in bed.

"I know you're tired," I say. "But I think you're overreacting."

"I think you're forgetting the agreement."

"Fuck the agreement."

My knees hit the hardwood floor. I feel wetness drip from my nose, and when it lands on my top lip, I know I'm bleeding.

Grant flips on the lamp. "Jesus, Josie."

I scoot away as he rounds the bed. He reaches me, leans down and takes me by the chin. He carefully inspects my face. I let him. I don't know to do anything different. He's never hit me before. I can't breathe. My vision is blurred. Finally, he exhales. "Well, at least it's not broken. Just a small cut where my ring got you."

When I can manage, I stand and start to throw my clothes in a bag. Mentally, I run down a list of items I'll need for James. I've reached my underwear drawer when he grabs me by the hair. "Where do you think you're going?"

"Away," I tell him through tears. I hadn't realized I was crying. Anger buries emotion.

"You can't leave," he laughs. "Where would you go?"

I try to maneuver away. "Anywhere but here."

"Look, Josie." He holds his hands up. "I feel bad for grazing your nose. But it was dark. I couldn't see."

I cock my head.

His eyes plead with me. I see remorse where irritation once was. "I feel terrible," he says, taking my hand in his. "But when you said that about the church— about everything I've worked so hard for—well, it was like you just obliterated everything we've built into nothing."

I back away. Suddenly, distance seems like a good thing.

"Come to bed," he says. "It's late. If you still want to leave in the morning, go right ahead. But don't drag our son out into the night just because you're angry. Can't you see I feel guilty enough already? Don't use him to make me feel worse."

"Josie," Mel calls. "Perhaps you should lie down here instead."

I wave her off. "I'm fine."

"Well," she says, handing me a bottle of water for the road. "If you're sure."

I wet my lips and focus on my breath. *In and out. In and out.* I inhale, stretching my arms out. They feel heavy. I roll my shoulders. She's right. I should lie down. I feel sick.

"I'm sorry," I say. "I think the sushi I had last night may have been bad."

She looks at me with concern. It's mostly fake. She just wants me out of her house before she has a mess to clean up.

"You keep dozing off..."

I twist the cap off the water and take a sip. "Just dehydrated is all."

Mel looks away. Her expression turns sad. "I used to get panic attacks too. They can be very scary."

"Panic attacks?"

"You know, kind of like flashbacks."

"No," I shake my head, and then I pat my stomach. "Just bad food is all."

I start toward the door. This isn't good. Beth will be all over this. She'll dissect my actions with a fine tooth comb. I'll be shifted off to another job. Back to meal duty. At least this way all I have to do is talk. New Hope is big enough now that typically we leave the other hospitality stuff to the others. Unless we're being punished.

"I hope you feel better," she calls from the entryway.

"Me too," I say over my shoulder. My stomach turns. Like the others, I came prepared to hate her.

I guess I half- expected that she would be some evil husband thief, but that isn't what she is at all.

She's just a young girl in over her head, with one big reason to stay. I know that reason. I know it well.

CHAPTER TWENTY-TWO

IZZY

I awake to the scent of bacon. Grant isn't in bed beside me. I pull the sheet in tighter. I could get used to this. I get used to waking up with nowhere I have to be and nothing I have to do. I search the floor for my clothes. There's a chill in the air that tells me better than to venture out unprotected. It makes me want to stay put. Bacon and Grant Dunn are sirens though, calling me, beckoning me toward them. Finally, I spot the lingerie from last night laid out at the end of the bed. I'd rather go naked than prance out wearing that in the daylight, looking like this. I don't think Grant Dunn has seen me fully sans clothing in the daylight. It's still too early for that. I stand, pull the sheet from the bed, and wrap it around me.

In the kitchen, Grant sits at the bar scrolling through his phone. "Good morning," I say.

He nods in response. He's immersed.

I scan the cabin. "Have you seen my suitcase?"

He looks up then. "Yes, but you won't be needing it."

"You might like me a little if I brush my teeth," I snort.

He frowns. "I'm a physician, Isobel. We don't do things willy-nilly. We don't go without basic necessities..." He scoffs. "There's an extra toothbrush on the counter."

"Thanks," I say. He motions for me to sit down and I take the seat opposite him at the table.

He searches my face. "Eat."

Breakfast is all laid out. There's a small portion of eggs, one slice of bacon and a tiny flute of orange juice. I laugh because it looks like one of those fancy restaurant meals where there's nothing really on the plate. Like it's been made just for looks.

His jaw tightens. "You don't like eggs?"

"No, I love eggs." I glance over at his empty plate wondering why he asks.

"I hope you don't mind I've eaten."

"Not at all," I say. I search the cabin for a clock. "What time is it?"

"A quarter 'til seven," he tells me, moving his phone aside. "I let you sleep in. Wanted to assess your sleeping patterns."

"Sounds very doctorly."

He studies me for a moment. I can't tell what he's thinking. "I would like it if you put the corset back on, please."

I take a stab at my eggs and then I shrug. "Okay."

It isn't exactly comfortable but the fabric is like nothing I've ever felt. I want to make him happy. There are worse things one can be asked to wear, that's for sure. Like the apron that says *I'm here to serve* across the chest and proudly displays the Lucky's logo. I'll take pretty lingerie over that any day.

"The eggs are amazing," I mention between bites. Most things are in small doses.

"This is your future," he says. He stands, walks over to me, and takes the sheet. Every inch of me tenses. It's freezing. "You just have to let me take care of you, Isobel."

I smile. He kisses me hard. I forget about the cold.

∼

THE GUY WHO MANAGES THINGS, COMES AND LEAVES OUR MEALS ON the porch. He doesn't ring the bell, he doesn't have to. When I search the kitchen for a snack, Grant explains that meals are delivered at precisely seven a.m., noon and seven p.m. On the dot.

On our second day there, I search for my phone again. I don't want to ask Grant for it. I don't want him to think I'm not having a good time. Still, I want to check Instalook and also to make sure there are no messages from Stacey. I haven't taken an entire weekend off. Ever. Surely, there's something about the place she doesn't know. More than anything, it's killing me that I don't know what Josie is up to. I need to know what she does in her free time. Honestly, I'm so bored here I don't know what to do with myself, and it would be nice to know the kind of thing Grant likes.

"Have you seen my phone?" I ask when I can't stand it any longer. I've read the same Austin Home and Garden magazine three times. "It was here," I say, pointing at the bar.

"You don't need your phone," he tells me, staring at his own. "Let it be."

"It's about the shop," I say. "Work." I figure he must know a thing or two about that.

He flicks his hand. "Let it be."

"Stacey, the owner— she doesn't know how to run it."

He gives me the side eye. "That's her business."

"Yeah, but—" I watch as he massages his temples and I stop myself.

"You're going to have to learn, as well, whose business is whose."

I adjust the corset.

His eyes scan my body. "Just relax," he says. "That's what we're here for."

I do relax, because he isn't wrong and it would be nice for Stacey to learn to manage things on her own.

Later that afternoon I'm reading the same magazine for the

fourth time on the couch when he throws me a T-shirt, a pair of his boxers, and a hoodie. "Put that on. We're going for a run."

"A run?" I laugh. "I don't run..."

He gives me a tight-lipped smile. "You do now."

I'M GOING TO DIE. MY CHEST IS SEIZING UP. I CAN'T BREATHE. I don't know how far we've run into the woods, but I do know it wasn't very far before my side cramped and I go from a run, to a jog, to a mere hobble. My legs feel like jelly. The pain in my ribs feels like someone's jabbing at me with a fire poker. It's hot, and it's spreading. I have no idea why anyone would want to do this sort of thing for fun.

I stop and double over. "I haven't gotten this much exercise since junior high school, and maybe not even then."

"This is really bad news," Grant eyes me cautiously. I'm just glad he's trained in CPR. I think I'm going to need it. I expect him to laugh at me. I expect him to crack a joke. But he doesn't. When I push myself up and meet his eye, his expression is fixed. "Your health is poor."

I cock my head. He's serious. "I never get sick."

"It's just a matter of time," he counters. "And I should know, I'm a doctor."

"I can't go on," I tell him, panting. I sound like an asthmatic, when really he's right. I'm very out of shape. But who cares? The way I see it, there are only a few reasons to run and pleasure isn't one of them.

"I'll meet you back at the cabin," I say reaching for a tree. I need to ground myself. It feels like holding on will give me life. Oxygen. Balance. I grip it hard, like it's a lifeline. My stomach turns. I'm suddenly glad breakfast was sparse. I feel it creeping up my throat. "Seriously," I assure him. "Go. I'll be fine."

I hope he believes me. It's too early in our relationship for vomit.

I feel him behind me. "I'm not leaving you like this."

My breaths have become short and raspy. My pulse is thrumming in my ears. His mouth is on my neck. I feel him bite softly. I try to turn to him. My head is swimming. He holds me in place and slides the boxers down. The g-string remains in place. He hits my ass. Hard. I jump. There isn't much wiggle room.

This isn't funny. I feel dizzy.

"Grab your ankles," he orders, pushing my head toward my calves. I glance over my shoulder surprised to see that he isn't joking. "Now."

I do as he says. All the blood rushes to my head. The upside is it helps with the dizziness. He grips my hips hard, his fingertips dig into my skin. He enters me from behind.

"I'm going to get a workout in you one way or another."

He grunts several thrusts in. I squeeze my eyes shut. I'm afraid my head is going to hit the tree. I'm afraid I'm going to collapse. Last night wasn't like this. Our first time as hurried as it was, wasn't like this. But I shouldn't complain. Chasing that high is what I said I wanted and it seems Grant Dunn knows how to do it.

"Don't worry," he mumbles. "I'll be quick."

It isn't a lie. When he's done, he turns me around to face him. I think he's going to explain, to ask me if I liked it. I think he's going to kiss me, take me in his arms. But he doesn't. "You'll be okay finding your way back then?"

I swallow hard. "Of course."

I watch as he turns and runs in the opposite direction and then I pick his boxers up off the ground and shake the leaves and dirt from them. I slide them on and backtrack to the cabin.

~

GRANT IS GONE FOR A LONG WHILE, SO LONG THAT I BEGIN TO worry he's gotten lost or hurt.

When he finally returns, just before dusk, he's quiet. He doesn't say where he's been. In fact, he really doesn't speak at all.

"I was worried," I say sidling up to him. I've showered and fixed my hair and makeup. I managed to locate my suitcase. But not my phone.

"You shouldn't have been," he tells me, stepping away. "I know these woods like the back of my hand."

"Is something wrong?" I ask after he's showered and shaven. I've tidied the cabin, made the bed and put on a pot of tea. "Yes," he answers. "I made a terrible mistake."

This is it. This is where it ends. Josie found out. That or she posted something on Instalook that made him second guess his decision. Probably a shot of her running. I should have given it more effort. This is why people end up alone. Laziness.

"Here," he says handing me a glass of water. He takes my hand in his and turns it over. "Take this."

I stare at the pill in the center of my palm.

"It's the morning after pill."

I scrunch my nose. "It's fine," I say. "I'm on birth control." It's a white lie. Still. It's doubtful he has anything to worry about.

"I want it to be extra fine," he replies lifting my hand, sliding it toward my face.

I mimic his shrug, pop the pill in my mouth and swallow. I don't even need the water.

"Thank you." I study his face, the satisfaction written all over it. It's so nice to see him happy again I'm not expecting what he says next. "I'm very worried, Isobel. About what happened in the woods."

"It's fine," I say again. I assume he's talking about the way he fucked me. Like an animal.

"It's not fine. You pushed me into doing something I wasn't ready to do." He sighs and turns away. He walks over to the kitchen window. He places his hands on the counter and leans all of his weight against them. He lets his head hang. "I can't resist you. And that," he says, "really scares me."

I narrow my gaze.

He continues. "We shouldn't have had unprotected sex. I've taken a risk. A huge risk."

"I'm clean. I—"

He turns then. "I've seen the kind of men who hang around you."

I do a double-take. "I—"

"The risk to me is very small," he interrupts. "It's there. However the risk of transmission is much higher for you." He widens his stance and folds his arms. I'm a child, and he stands over me. There are things he's warned me about, his expression says, but sometimes you can't learn until you suffer the consequences. He takes a deep breath in and lets it out. "You should be more careful with your body, Isobel. Offering it up so freely—well, I have to say—that concerns me."

My eyes grow wide. I feel sick. "I—"

He places his finger to my lips effectively cutting me off. "No point in worrying now. What's done is done."

Tears have welled up in my eyes. I blink them back. Hold them in. They run out the sides anyway. Grant shakes his head and leaves the cabin.

〜

THIS TIME HE RETURNS SOONER. AND WITH FLOWERS. "NO LILIES this time," he chuckles offering them to me. "It's slim pickings way out here." He leans down and kisses my cheek. He's chipper. A different man than the one who left the cabin earlier. I want to leave. I hate to ask. It only proves my guilt.

"I'm sorry to worry you," he tells me, opening the fridge. I watch as he removes a bottle of champagne. "Like I said, you scare me." He places it on the counter and glances in my direction. "The way I feel about you—" He pauses and shakes his head. He looks away. "You know what?"

I don't, but I want to. My eyes are on his. He's on stage, and I'm captivated by the performance.

He breaks out in full grin. "How about we save that conversation for later? Let's eat. I bet you're starving..."

I nod. But I don't say anything. I don't know what to say.

"How well do you know the Bible?" he asks as he readies dinner.

I would have done it, but I wasn't sure when he was coming back. I want to tell him this but nothing sounds right in my head so I don't.

He raises his brow, and I realize he's waiting for an answer.

"Probably not well enough."

"There's one in the drawer there. Instead of that magazine," he motions. "You might consider switching it up a bit."

I press my lips together.

"Do you regret coming?" he asks. His face grows solemn. "I realize I'm intense Isobel. I know it can be too much for some people. Especially so soon..."

I narrow my gaze. Suddenly, I hone in on the flowers and the bottle of champagne he's holding.

"I—"

"Wait—" he says suspending one hand in the air. "I hope you like strawberries."

"Yes," I tell him. I don't regret coming. I don't want him to feel bad. Not after all of this.

He wipes the back of his hand across his forehead. "Whew," he says laughing playfully. "So, you aren't ready to head for the hills?"

I shake my head. "I'm having a great time."

～

"Izzy," Grant says waking me from sleep. I groan. I think he wants sex again. I'm sore. He's a machine. "Izzy," he calls shaking my shoulder. "Please explain this."

I open my eyes. He's holding my phone. My heart races. I panic.

He tosses the phone in my direction. "Maybe I was right," he says pacing the length of the bedroom. "Maybe this is too much too soon..."

"What do you mean?" I ask, wiping the sleep from my eyes, even though I'm so awake my hair stands on end.

He sighs long and heavy. He isn't angry. He's sad. "I just don't think you're that serious about being with me..."

"Of course, I'm serious," I say. My throat constricts, and I ball my fists. Flex them a few times. I feel it building, that familiar feeling, and try to stuff it down. I don't know what he's seen. I force myself to remember what I deleted. It helps that I have a shit phone with zero memory. So I hope most of it.

"Then why are you texting that guy? Just last week. And more importantly, why is he texting you asking if he can come over?"

"He's my friend."

"Bullshit." His voice comes out harsh and sudden.

Lie even if they catch you red-handed. Remain faithful to your lies even in the face of overwhelming evidence. I meet his gaze, letting a small smirk convey the simmering fury. Rage is important when you're trying to conceal the truth. "You're the one who's married."

He slaps the wall hard. A painting falls to the floor. Losing your temper can be an expensive mistake. We both stare at it. Eventually, he shakes his head and leaves the room. He leaves things where they are. I try harder. I take a few deep breaths. *Focus on blue, I hear the voice say. Don't let them break you.*

"I knew it was a matter of time before you brought that up," he calls from the other room. I ignore him and go into the bathroom and splash cold water on my face. I have to get myself in check. I don't want Grant to see this side of me. He won't understand.

I run the water and I sit on the edge of the tub. I hold my breath and count to ten. I hear him speaking, but my head is spinning. I'm five again and on a merry-go-round and I want off. I don't want to hear what he's saying. I put my head between my knees. Blue. Blue is all I see.

Eventually, I hear the front door open and close

Grant doesn't come back for the rest of the night. I know because I don't sleep. I toss and I turn. And I wait.

THE NEXT MORNING I FIND HIM IN THE KITCHEN HUMMING, MAKING pancakes. I dozed off sometime just after dawn.

"Grant," I say leaning against the counter. "I'm sorry about last night," I tell him. I've had a lot of time to think. He's right about Tyler. He isn't good for me. "I shouldn't have mentioned your wife —it's really none of my business."

He doesn't respond, and he doesn't look at me. He doesn't even stop humming. He's focused on the pancakes. "Timing is everything, Izzy. One second too long over the heat, and these babies will be useless to us."

I don't know what he means but I don't care. I need to make this right. I need to make peace. "I think you were right before." He looks up. I laugh nervously. "I need to learn whose business is whose."

"You're right about that," he agrees. He nods for me to come closer. I stand on my tippy-toes and kiss him full on the mouth.

He pulls away. "Timing," he smiles. I watch as he tosses the cooked pancakes onto a plate. "And now that we're both clear where the other stands, it's all good."

I exhale slowly. I hop up on the counter beside where he works. I study his capable hands. He moves like music. Like a symphony.

"Plus," he tells me, moving closer. "It's our last day together, we might as well make the most of it." He presses a bit of batter to the tip of my nose.

I don't know what he means by last day together. I don't know whether he means here at the cabin or in general. The scary part is, it could be either. Which is why I vow right then and there to make this the best day ever so that it won't be our last. I need him to want more. I'm not ready to go back to that lonely apartment, or that dead end job, or Tyler and his boyish sex. I'll work on my issues. All of them. Even the ones he doesn't know about.

"You shouldn't underestimate me, Grant Dunn," I say playfully.

He cocks his head, his fingers never stop working their magic. "I'd like to hear about your work," I say. "About the way you make things beautiful."

He nods. But he doesn't say anything further. So I don't either. But that doesn't stop me from thinking. I'm ready to be serious. Finally, someone wants that for me— he wants that for us.

CHAPTER TWENTY-THREE

JOSIE

It's true. Absence does make the heart grow fonder. Grant returns from his weekend at the cabin more relaxed than I've ever seen him. That Monday, he surprises Avery by personally taking her to school. He has his attorney meet them there. They have no proof that she's harassed anyone, and I don't know exactly what was said, but I know a formal apology was issued.

I post it on Instalook. People appreciate knowing what I've been dealing with. They're appalled on my behalf, and it makes me realize I have been dealing with a lot. I wasn't imaging it.

Monday evening Grant comes home at a decent hour and announces he's taking me to dinner. He doesn't tell me what to wear, but seems pleased by my choice. He doesn't request sex, and when I offer the usual blow job instead, he surprises me with a bracelet.

"Do you like it?" he asks earnestly. "I wasn't sure it was your style."

"I love it," I tell him. It's the truth.

He watches me reapply my makeup. "Aren't you going to show it off to your friends?"

I shake my head. "I'm thinking of taking a break from the

internet." This is partly true, but also, I've received so many comments and messages about the Avery/bully situation and how everything is taken so far these days that it seems odd to brandish jewelry at a time like this.

He looks concerned.

"You look nice," I say, adjusting his tie. I don't know where he's taking me, he hasn't said, but dressed like this, I know it's somewhere good.

"What's up with the break?" he asks with a nod and I should have known it wouldn't be that easy.

"I just want to focus more on what's important."

His eyebrows raise. "Your happiness is important, is it not?"

I feel an argument coming on. We haven't argued in nearly a week. Maybe longer. "You make me happy," I tell him. I want to continue the good streak.

"Yes," he smiles. "But so does your—what do you call them —your tribe?"

"Oh," I say, waving him off. I half snort. "You know that's mostly for the church— the reason I share so much—but—" I pause. I've already said too much. I don't want to talk about the church or any of that right now. That part, I'm saving for later.

He cocks his head. "But what?"

"I don't know." I search for my shoes. "It just sort of started to feel like a job."

"People depend on you, Josie. You lift them up. You give them hope. So, in that way it is sort of a job."

He's stroking my ego, and I have to admit I kind of like it. I spot my heels. "You're right," I say, slipping them on. "Here," I say pausing to hand him my phone. "Can you take it?"

He smiles. It takes more effort than one realizes trying to get a decent shot with one hand. He does a good job. But then, he's good with his hands. I filter it anyway. Night on the town with my man, I caption it. #bestsurpriseever

〜

"Josie," he says grabbing my wrist. My eyes follow his grip. "You forgot the bracelet."

"Shit," I say. My mouth forms a hard line. I glance toward the house. "I took it off when we made love."

"Yes." He smiles. "I remember."

I take my phone from my clutch. I haven't seen my husband this happy in ages. "I'll have Avery run it out."

"Don't." He places his hand on the phone. "I'll get it."

I watch as he jogs through the front door. I check Instalook. One thousand and thirty-four likes so far on my photo. My audience has grown significantly over the weekend. Maybe my husband is right. Maybe a break isn't what I need. I snap a photo of my new nail color and post it for good measure. I specifically don't mention the color so people will ask. Engagement is everything. Grant emerges from the house. He stops on the top step and holds the bracelet up triumphantly. I throw my head back and laugh. Maybe I won't discuss my decision with him tonight after all. Maybe it can wait.

"Ready?" he asks after he clasps the bracelet around my wrist. He brings it to his lips.

I nod.

He puts the car in reverse. I respond to the comments on my nails. It's midnight blue.

"People really shouldn't park on the street," he says, pouncing on the brake abruptly. "It's against HOA rules."

I look up from my phone. "I think they're just waiting," I tell him craning my neck. "See. There's someone in the car."

"Well then," he mumbles. I look over. He's squinting, trying to get a better look. My husband hates to be wrong. "I wish they'd wait somewhere else."

"Where are we headed?" I inquire, changing the subject.

"Downtown," he says. He meets my eye. His jaw is set. "Call Avery and ask her to make sure I locked the front door, please."

I'm replying to a comment. I remember I'd forgotten to go back in and tag the photo with the nail polish brand. Sometimes they send me free stuff. This will help. "Do it now," he says, sternly. It causes me to jump. I tap out of Instalook. He swings the car around and then looks over at me. He presses his lips to one another. "Never mind. I'll just go back and check myself."

I'VE CHECKED THE CAKE AND THE CATERER AND THE GIFT TABLE. I'VE laid out napkins and inspected the wine glasses for smudges. "This is a big deal," Grant says. He can see my concern. He wants everything to be perfect too. "How many times does your son turn sixteen?"

"Just once," I smile.

"You look beautiful," he says. He's not looking at me, though.

"I don't like this top," I say later, checking myself in the mirror. Everything is about presentation. "I think I'm going to change."

He looks up then. I know what he's thinking. Any minute now, the first of our guests will begin arriving. "We're expecting forty people any second now." He glances at his wrist. "The top is fine."

I straighten it. I've lost weight, thanks to the added workouts and the stress with Avery. Nothing fits right.

"Have you given any consideration to my suggestion?"

"I don't want surgery."

"Breast augmentations are very common for women your age." I think of June.

He reads my mind. "What happened with June was very rare, Jos."

I remove the top. He studies me carefully. I can see the wheels in his mind turning. He reaches out and cups my left breast.

184

"Hmmm," he mutters. Nothing more. It says enough. I don't have to ask what he's thinking. I know.

"You're lovely," he tells me. He lies. "Here, I think you should wear this one," he says handing me a blouse from the stack lying on the bed. It's beige, and it tells me what he wants from me today. He wants me to blend in. This is what happens when you spend decades with a person. You don't question them because you want to know why they want what they want. You question them because you need to know you want the same.

"What's going on with you?" I ask. He seems nervous. Especially lately. Different, too. Not that I'm complaining.

"There's nothing wrong," he assures me. "I just have a lot on my mind. Work."

I think of our son and his birthday and our guests. "I'm sorry," I say. I don't quite know what I'm sorry for. For the last few months, for being so distracted lately, for not being more appreciative, for all of it, perhaps.

∼

"YOU DID GOOD," MY HUSBAND TELLS ME, SLIPPING HIS ARM AROUND my waist.

I smile. "Remind me again why we didn't have this at the clubhouse?"

He pulls me close and plants a kiss on the top of my head. We stand together watching the commotion as friends fill our backyard. "This is our home," he says. "It should be this way."

I take a glass of wine from a server's tray.

"Plus," he adds, squeezing my waist. "It's nice to have our friends here. Our job is to unify and grow the congregation. What better place to do it than our home?"

"You're right," I whisper leaning into him.

He glances at me sideways. "You really are a lot smarter than I give you credit for."

"Nice to know," I say playfully. I jab his gut. Laughter breaks out. Our eyes follow. Beth and her husband are talking to the Bennetts. Tom and Mel have a small group around them, and the rest of our closest friends from New Hope are pittering about, enjoying the hors d'oeuvres. It's the kids laughing. James is telling a story. I strain to hear, but there's too much chatter to make out specifics.

"It is important to show the newcomers hospitality—" Grant says getting my attention. "You know, what an ideal family looks like. It gives them something to aspire to."

I do know. Which is why I still haven't told him I want out. My husband is particular about change. I realize I'm going to have to plead my case. Somehow, I don't think this is the appropriate time.

Eventually, he pats my backside. "Go on," he says. "Mingle."

I down the last of my wine and mentally tally how many of these people will still be around when we leave the church. None.

He places his hand on the small of my back and pushes me into the crowd. "Social affairs are meant to be social."

HALFWAY THROUGH THE PARTY, GRANT CUTS IN VIA THE SOUND system.

"May I have your attention?" His eyes scan the crowd. He's looking for me. I've always loved my husband's face most when he doesn't realize I'm watching. He commands everyone's attention.

His eyes land on mine and his face lights up. "First, I want to thank my beautiful wife for putting this all together," he says raising his glass. "I'll never know how I got so lucky."

Our friends cheer. There's clapping. Someone whistles.

"Secondly, I'd like to thank you all for coming. This community means everything to us. And I do mean everything." He looks to me for confirmation. A lump forms in my throat. It hits me. It's there, the truth in his expression. Leaving New Hope with his blessing is never going to happen.

I smile and look away, shyly.

"Also, to my son. James— What a lucky man I have been to see you grow into the young man you've become. I couldn't be more proud."

I feel tears brimming my eyelids. I watch my husband. I don't want to give him up. His shoulders drop. His face relaxes. "To family and friends."

I hold up my wine glass and repeat after him. "To family and friends."

Mel is standing beside me. "You really are the luckiest," she says, beaming. Her hand rests on her still flat stomach.

"The luckiest," I agree.

She gasps and turns to face me full on, as though she's about to share the depths of her soul. "I can't wait to find out what we're having." She lowers her voice. "Tom says he doesn't want to know. But I think he'll come around. Otherwise, I have no idea how I'll keep a secret like that from him. Can you imagine?"

"No," I say. Then I remember. I'm supposed to talk with her. Grant will ask if I set it up. "Do you have time for tea on Tuesday?"

"Tea sounds perfect," she smiles. She lightly touches my arm when she speaks. She trusts me. She has no idea.

※

"THESE ARE FOR YOU," GRANT SAYS TO OUR SON. I CAN'T SEE WHAT he's holding from where I'm standing but I can guess. He presses the button on the garage.

James covers his mouth. "NO WAY. A Volvo."

Grant looks at me and grins. The model he has chosen is one of the safest cars around. He slaps our son on the back and then makes his way over to where I'm standing. "Now," he says leaning in. His lips graze my ear. "You don't have to worry so much."

He's wrong.

"I have another surprise," he announces. "One that's more for you."

James comes from behind and throws his arms around me. "Thanks, mom." I turn and pull him into a hug. He's taller than me, has been for a while, and it's awkward. "You have your dad to thank," I tell him, and then he's off, obviously thrilled, as any kid his age would be. My eyes find my daughter. She's standing against the car trying not to look as envious as she feels.

I walk over to where she stands. She pulls out her phone. "It'll be your turn soon," I say.

She chews her lip and stares at the pavement.

"Plus," I say pulling her in close. "I have a surprise for you tomorrow." I'm taking her shopping. She's been so withdrawn lately. She's retreated into herself, to a place I can't reach.

She looks at me and offers a small smile. Fourteen is rough. Everyone says that. Grant told me the other night at dinner I shouldn't worry so much. He doesn't know what it's like to be someone's mother. He doesn't have to. He doles out worries. I handle them.

"Cake," Grant says slinging his arm around Avery's shoulder. "Let's have cake."

She crosses her arms and plants her feet. "I hate cake."

"Envy isn't very becoming," he murmurs. This time she goes with him.

I watch as they walk toward the house, his arm still slung over her shoulder. "Just think." I hear him say. "By the time you're driving, your mom will have relaxed a bit. You won't have to have a safe car."

"Yeah, right."

He glances back at me. I raise my brow. "Yeah, right," I say.

Back inside, the party resumes. "It's almost time for the grand finale," Grant whispers in my ear.

"The grand finale wasn't the car?"

He bites the tip of my ear lobe. "You shouldn't underestimate me, Mrs. Dunn."

∼

"I'M SO PROUD OF YOU FOR LOSING THE WEIGHT," HE TOLD ME THE other night over dinner. "I wasn't sure you had it in you."

"I told you," I said picking at my salad. "It was just my period."

He shakes his head, reaches for my hand, and rubs my fingers. "I'm just so glad we're finally on the same page."

I brace myself. I can tell there's something more. I get the feeling he's going to bring up the agreement. "Speaking of which —" he starts. I hold my breath. "I need to ask you a favor."

I tilt my head. A waiter refills our water glass and then lifts the champagne bottle from the ice. I haven't eaten much, so I'm grateful for the buzz. Grant shoos him off before he has a chance to refill my glass.

His eyes meet mine. "I need you to talk with Mel."

"Mel?"

He glances away before leaning in. "She isn't holding up her end of the bargain."

I'm confused. "What bargain?"

"Tom says she isn't…um…you know…as willing…"

I understand then what he's asking of me.

"She's pregnant."

"Yes, I'm aware." He purses his lips. "Tom thinks she trapped him."

I scoff. "Well, Tom shouldn't have slept with her if Tom didn't want to be trapped."

I reach for the champagne. He holds his palm up facing me.

"That's not the point. As her mentor, it's your job to see that she's adhering to the agreement." He replaces the bottle to its rightful place. My glass remains empty. "I need you to help her understand."

"I don't see—"

"Josie," he interrupts. "Tom is adamant that she—" he pauses and lowers his voice. "Otherwise his tithe will be lower. We can't afford for that to happen. "

"She's pregnant," I remind him again. "No one feels like being at someone's beck and call when they're pregnant."

"It's her duty," he says firmly. "How do you think she got that way?"

A PHOTO OF ME PREGNANT, VERY PREGNANT IN FACT, FLASHES ON the screen. We all gather around a projector in our backyard. Grant has put together a slideshow. This isn't like him. He isn't crafty, and under normal circumstances he isn't sentimental.

Another photo replaces it. I remember Grant taking this one. It was the night before James was born. We'd placed bets on when I'd go into labor and with each passing day, it seemed as though I might stay pregnant forever. I hear laughter. I look over at our daughter. She's mortified to see proof that her parents do indeed have sex. "You were huge," she says. "And so young."

I was happy. Another photo of Grant in the delivery room pops up. He's giving the thumbs up. He looked happy. Naive. Different. I guess we both were. I want to feel nostalgic, instead I feel something else. It's stirring. Building.

"Look," Avery says pointing to the screen. "Look how cute he was then." I do look. It's a photo of James taking his first bite of real food. He doesn't know what to make of it. His face is twisted. I'm laughing. That was before I believed anything bad could happen. Before I understood life could turn on a dime. It was before all the rules, before New Hope. Before.

I think of Mel. I'm dreading Tuesday. I look over at her. She's about to get her first taste of the far reaches of the church, and I hate to be the one to deliver it.

Someone laughs across the room. When I glance back at the screen, James is blowing out birthday candles on his first birthday cake and then every year after that. As pictures, one after the other, flash on the screen, I forget about Mel and New Hope. My eyes well up, and tears spill over. Grant beams. This is the reaction he wanted. There are vacations and school photos. There are photos of us napping and reading, and I can see my husband back behind the lens, back before capturing the perfect photo became so important. Before filters and coming up with the perfect captions. Back when he took them because he wanted to. When it was okay to be ordinary. Before we had anything to prove.

"HERE," GRANT SAYS, HANDING BETH MY PHONE. "TAKE A PHOTO OF us. Would you?"

She arranges Avery next to Grant, James next to me. "Scooch in."

"Now, switch," she tells them, biting her lip, lining up the phone.

"Haven't we taken enough photos?" James sighs.

I laugh impatiently.

Beth rolls her eyes. "Didn't your parents just buy you a car?" She shakes her head. "Smile."

Someone spills their drink across the room. It's sudden chaos.

She snaps a photo and then checks my phone to make sure it's a good one. "Nope," she says frowning.

We take three more and then another. None are good enough.

Finally, around the seventh try the kids protest and we disband. "The last one was perfect," Beth exclaims pleased with herself.

"You've done well here, Josie," she tells me afterward. I smile. It takes a lot to get a sincere compliment out of her. "We need to talk about our social strategy," she tells me, taking my elbow. She takes my phone from my back pocket. "We need more of this," she says pulling up the photo. "This is what they want. To see behind the scenes. So—" she shrugs. "Might as well give it to them."

"I was just telling Josie that last night," Grant remarks. "She doesn't realize how important her work on social media is." I look over at him and offer a tight smile.

I glance down at the photo. My eyes are still glossy from the slideshow. The kids look happy. Things get more real around the seventh shot apparently. Still, their friends are here, Avery is smiling again. Grant's expression says he's taking it all in, contemplating how lucky he is.

"I do realize," I say uploading it to Instalook. "See."

He smiles as he brings the phone closer to his face inspecting it with a surgeon's eye. Finally, he nods his approval, and I can see why. We look so happy, the four of us. Beth has framed it up so well that I don't even bother using a filter. I caption it #bestdayever. I had no idea, not then, it would be the last best day.

CHAPTER TWENTY-FOUR

IZZY

I shouldn't have gone the first time. I knew I shouldn't have. But once I'd made the decision, it was done. It's kind of like telling yourself you're only going to have one potato chip and then the next thing you know the bag is empty. That's how it started. Just one peek, I promised myself. I mean, Josie Dunn had invited me there herself initially. Before. When things were so good, I had to cancel. Before Grant Dunn was too busy to return a simple text.

The other night I sat outside their house for hours. I watched the Dunns come and go. I had to. I needed to see for myself. Grant says he's busy this time of year. It wasn't a lie.

He has been busy.

Busy buying his wife earrings, and taking her to dinner. Busy throwing parties. But not busy keeping the promises he made to me. He said he wanted to get to know everything about me. He said he wanted to take care of me. Only he isn't busy doing any of that.

I feel like you're forgetting what you promised, I texted him.

How could I forget someone so beautiful? He wrote back six hours later. Six hours.

At first, I was relieved to see his name light up my screen. Then I remembered flattery is his currency. He doles it out like breadcrumbs. It isn't genuine. I can't believe him. He lies about everything.

~

JOSIE DUNN IS GROCERY SHOPPING. SHE POSTED A PIC OF FLOWERS in her cart on Instalook three minutes ago. This means I don't have long. I tell myself it's fine being here. I was invited. Maybe not this time but if anything, I'll just say there was a mix up. I'll say I thought we'd rescheduled the dance lesson. Everyone knows teenagers get things wrong.

I check my reflection in the rearview mirror. My phone rings startling me. My heart races every time I hear that sound. It might be Grant.

It isn't. It's Tyler. I want to slam it into a million pieces. What good is it if the person you want to call isn't? Not much.

I send the call to voicemail. I know what he wants. He wants his car back. I've been gone too long again. The last time I got by with a blow job. This time, I had to go through with the whole thing and then wait until he was asleep. It's not even a nice car.

But you do what you have to do. Josh taught me that. Anyway, it was worth it, I realize, being here. I can breathe again knowing I'm one step closer. I've been suffocating under the weight of Grant's absence, and then there were the Instalook posts of the kid's birthday party. I didn't know what to do, looking at them. I drove over. I wanted to be a part of things. I wanted Grant to welcome me inside. He had no reservations about setting up shop inside me, coming inside me. Making me erase his baby before it even had a chance. That's okay. I didn't want 'maybe baby' either.

What I want is him. What I want is for Josie to understand. I'm not stupid. I realize it will take some time. I know women don't just let go of their men like it's nothing. Believe me, I know.

But this time it could be different. We could be friends. Times have changed. We could do that thing everyone is doing these days where we co-parent. They could consciously uncouple. We could celebrate holidays together, take a vacation or two. It always works out in the end. And if it hasn't worked out, it isn't the end.

I mean, I don't really like kids. But hey, like they say, you can't help who you fall in love with.

In any case, I can see that things will need some sorting out. Maybe it isn't that Grant is busy. Maybe he isn't good at logistics. And why would he be? He has people to work all that out for him. Also, they say transitions are the hardest part. Maybe he just hasn't grown into himself yet.

Me, I'm changing. I apply lip-gloss to drive home the point. It's the kind I saw Josie tag on Instalook. I got a manicure, too. Midnight blue. Now, I just have to make her understand. It's not that I want her out of the picture. I think there's room for all of us.

~

"James?" I cock my head, narrow my eyes. He opens the door a little wider when I say his name.

He's studying me intently trying to place my face. "I'm Izzy," I say extending my hand. He's Grant, only younger. We shake on it. He's polite. Maybe all kids aren't as bad as I've made them out to be. Maybe it won't be as hard as I think to accept this kind of baggage. "I'm here to give Avery her dance lesson."

He raises his brow and removes an earbud from his ear. He wasn't even listening. I could be anyone. They're those new cordless kind; I hardly noticed. "Avery's out back," he tells me, stepping aside. I guess he reads lips. He points. "In the studio."

"Ah," I say following him in. "I guess she got a head start."

I follow him through the house to the back door. I could probably find my way if I wanted to. I know it from Instalook, I know every room. I've studied it. Designed the layout in my mind. I wasn't far off. Except the kitchen—it's bigger than I thought. I have lived and breathed these rooms. I have imagined myself sitting, loving, sleeping beneath this roof, and now here I am. I follow him onto the patio.

He points. "In there."

"Thanks," I say. I take a deep breath in and let it out. Gosh. This is so much easier than I thought. All you have to do is act like you belong. Like you're meant to be. So long as you look and act the part they want you to play, people are much more accepting than you imagine. This is why I'm wearing the workout gear I'm wearing. It's why I got eyelash extensions and a blow out. I maxed out my credit card. But here I am, standing in the center of the Dunns' world. Who knew it would be as simple as that?

SHE SITS CROSS-LEGGED ON THE FLOOR WITH HEADPHONES OVER HER ears. I watch as she bobs her head to the beat. She looks different in her own environment. More sure of herself when she doesn't know anyone's watching. Most of us are. You could be my step-child.

I lean against the wall, placing one foot up behind me. She senses movement and she looks up. Unlike her brother, she knows my face. She lifts the headphones. I watch as she places them on the floor. There's something in her expression that reminds me of Josie. I can't place exactly what that something is. "Did you forget?" I ask, checking my new watch. It's the kind everyone is posting on Instalook. It's expensive and edgy. Seems like something a girl like her would appreciate.

She shrugs. "My mom probably forgot to tell me."

I roll my eyes. "Moms."

She almost snickers, and her youth shows. We talk about dance stuff for a bit and then I work with her on technique. Once we're both properly sweating, me more than her, I go in for the kill. "So—" I say, careful to choose the right words. Kids are better than adults at picking up on deception. That's why I don't like them. "What exactly happened with the dance team? You seem pretty good. It doesn't make sense why they would cut you."

She looks away.

When she doesn't answer, I plop down on the hardwood floor. I don't really know anything about dance. I lied. My mom never owned a studio. What I do know is how the click of a few tabs on the internet can open up whole new worlds. "Show me your latest routine."

After several moments she complies.

"Yeah," I say again. "It makes no sense why they'd cut you. At my school—with your talent—you would have been captain."

"Exactly," she says rolling her eyes. "Someone wanted the lead. I guess that someone found a way to get it…"

"That happens sometimes."

She looks at me then as though she and I share a secret, some unspoken portal into the workings of the universe.

She stops after practicing several turns. "They expelled me over it."

My eyes grow wide. I hadn't realized that part. Maybe I should cut Grant some slack. His kid is a delinquent. "Like kicked out of school—expelled?"

"Yeah, for something I didn't even do."

I lean back on my palms and scan the room. Then I look at her directly. "Wow…"

She studies herself in the mirror. I can tell she doesn't like what she sees. Girls her age never do. "What should I do about it?"

"What does your mom say?"

She scoffs. "My mom. I haven't told her."

"Surely, she knows you were expelled?"

"Oh, she knows."

"Really."

She moves closer to the mirror and studies her face. "Yeah, she knows about that. But the rest of it—" she says, picking at something she'd be better off leaving alone. I would tell her, but sometimes it's nice to hold back. People rarely listen to warnings anyway. "She doesn't know about the rest of it."

"Oh." I consider what to say next. I can't tell her I know about the messages, even if I do. I especially can't tell her it was me who sent them. I chew at my bottom lip trying to find a way around it.

"Why don't you tell her?"

"The truth?" She eyes me like I'm an alien that's just landed in her studio. She thought she knew me. Now she realizes she doesn't know me at all. "God, no," she says. "That would cause all kinds of problems."

"And your dad?"

She gives me a funny look. God, I have so much to teach her. More than dance I learned on the internet, that much is clear. In the meantime, it's good to let people think they're smarter than you. That way, they drop their guard. "What kind of problems? Maybe I can help."

"You mean like you'll tell my parents? Um... yeah. No. Thank you."

"No, I mean like give you advice. I'm not a parent. Thank God." I make sure my eyes bulge for good measure. Teenagers appreciate drama. So do grown women for that matter. "I don't even like kids, really."

She accepts the truth in my lie. "There's nothing I can do..." she confesses sadly. "They let me back in school. But now everyone treats me differently."

"There's always murder," I say. I should be careful. The power of suggestion is far-reaching.

She laughs. I do too.

"My friends abandoned me. I mean—" she starts and then she pauses. Her breath catches, and I can see Grant Dunn really does have his hands full. It's no wonder it takes him six hours to respond to a text. It takes half as long to get the truth out of his kid. He's still working at it.

It looks like she might cry, and God— I do hate kids. Finally, she takes a breath. "I can tell they think I did it."

I shrug. "Anyway. Who needs friends?"

She studies my face carefully. She can't tell if I'm serious. Eventually, she offers a tight smile.

"Anyway—you have me now."

I watch her eyes. They always give it away. I've said too much. Sometimes I like to apply a little pressure just to see how far I can get.

She turns toward the door. "My mom will be back soon."

"From work?" I ask, although I know Josie doesn't know real work.

She shakes her head. "No, from church."

"Your mom goes to church?" I already know the answer but details would be nice.

She furrows her brow. "She invited you. Remember?"

Shit. I bite my lip. Now, I've made her suspicious. "Yeah, I don't really like church."

"That's too bad," she says. "You might not want to mention that to my mom. She practically is the church."

That, I didn't know. "And your dad? Does he go too?"

"Are you kidding? He created religion."

I assume this is the teenager in her coming out. I don't know what to make of it. I recall the way her father bent me over in the woods. I remember the way he laid into me on the hood of his car, the way he pushed my head down in the kitchen at Lucky's, further and further, until there was no more give. Nothing seemed particularly religious about that. Maybe I don't know religion like I thought. That reminds me, I never took Josie up on her offer to get me to church. Now, I realize I need to rectify that.

❲

AVERY LEADS ME THROUGH THE HOUSE. SHE'S TAKING ME STRAIGHT through to the front door, I realize a tad too late.

"Say," I whisper. "Can I get a water for the road?"

She turns on her heel, like a ballerina and beckons me to follow.

Josie is in the kitchen putting away groceries. We catch her off guard. "Oh," she says, shoving a carton of OJ in their sub-zero fridge. "You."

She looks from her daughter to me and back. I can see she's wondering if she's forgotten something. "I didn't know you were coming—"

I jut my bottom lip out. Avery hands me the water. "Hmm, I—"

The door closes in another part of the house. I hear footsteps I can't see. Josie glances toward the front door. "It must have slipped my mind," she says. She presses her hand to her chest. She's not sure of herself. I can tell by the way she rolls her eyes. "Thank God you're not an axe murderer."

I narrow my gaze. "Me a murderer? No," I say. "Seems like a lot of work."

She laughs. Avery stares at her mother, her mouth open. She looks like most teenagers look when their parents have over-stayed their welcome in their presence. "What?" Josie laughs. "It was a joke."

I want to tell her, her joke isn't funny, but then Grant walks in. He has his phone in his hand. He's punching at the screen. I wait for him to look up. One Mississippi. Two Mississippi. Three Missi—.

I watch in amusement as he lets the phone go. Just like that, his fingers release it, and it goes crashing to the floor. Suddenly, all eyes are on me. But it's only Josie's expression that gives anything away.

CHAPTER TWENTY-FIVE

JOSIE

"Not another one," I say to Grant as he retrieves his undoubtedly cracked phone from the marble floor. Another grand down the drain, just like that. I wouldn't know this time, though. I'm looking at her. She meets my gaze briefly before turning her attention to my husband. I can't help but follow suit.

"Whoops," he says. His eyes are narrowed. His mouth contorted. He holds up the pieces of his lifeline to the world and suddenly it's show and tell. His lips part slowly. "Didn't expect to see anyone standing there."

Seeing his reaction, I feel dizzy. Faint. Sucker-punched. Like the wind has been knocked out of me. I thought I knew that feeling. But not like this. My eyes scan the room, they scan faces, bodies, they scan my whole life.

"I'm from the coffee shop," she smiles shyly. "Lucky's."

"Right," he says. The muscles in his jaw go slack. "I thought you looked familiar."

"She's working with Avery on some dance stuff," I say. I brace myself. There's been an earthquake, and it seems I'm the only one who felt it.

Grant cocks his head slowly. He's precise in his movements. Calculated. "You're a dancer?"

She blushes. "I used to be."

I grip the countertop. It's all there in the red of her cheeks. It isn't infatuation I see. I'm used to that when it comes to women and my husband. But this time there's more, a lot more, and as much as I want to, I can't not know anymore.

I LEAN AGAINST THE DOORFRAME AND WATCH MY HUSBAND BRUSH his teeth. I must have done this same thing dozens, if not hundreds of times over the years, but we both know this time is different. "How do you know Izzy?"

He knows it's coming. I can see it in the way his shoulders tense when he meets my gaze in the mirror. His brushing slows. My legs feel like jelly. *You've held it together this long. Breathe.* We've eaten dinner as a family, discussed the ins and outs of our days. I've helped with homework, signed permission slips, hugged my children. I've completed our normal routine as though nothing were amiss, as though the foundation of my life has not been ripped at the core.

"Who?" He spits foam into the sink and flips the faucet on. Everything sharpens. Nausea gnaws at my insides. My pulse throbs in my teeth. Maybe I'm wrong. Maybe the flush on her cheeks, the familiarity in their conversation, has an explanation. Maybe my husband likes coffee more than I thought.

Maybe I already know the truth.

"Izzy," I say speaking over the sound of the water. "The girl who was in our kitchen earlier." *The girl you've been fucking behind my back. The one I was stupid enough to invite into our lives when she'd clearly already had a place in yours.*

He spits another mouthful of foamy toothpaste into the sink and then meets my eye. "The girl from the coffee shop?"

I cock my head. *Did I not try hard enough? Where did I go wrong?*

"Do I know her?" he says drying his hands. "What is that supposed to mean?"

It means— how long have you been fucking her behind my back? How long have I, this life, been a joke to you? How did I not see that you wanted out? How did I misjudge her? It means—silly me. I hadn't assumed her pretty enough to grab your attention. Somehow I failed to see her youth, her eagerness to please, her perky tits. How is it I've become a part of a competition I never knew existed? "It means what I asked... do you know her or not?"

He turns and smiles with one side of his mouth. He takes a few steps forward. He shrugs, noncommittally. It makes sense given the context of the conversation. His smile fades. "I've talked with her a few times while waiting for my order. But I'd hardly say that qualifies as knowing her." He doesn't admit he's slept with her. But he doesn't outright lie either. There's safety in the gray area. He's smart that way. He knows there's not much you can do with the in between.

CHAPTER TWENTY-SIX

IZZY

"I can't believe you would come to my home, Isobel," Grant says pacing the length of Lucky's. Back and forth, back and forth. He stops suddenly and pinches the bridge of his nose. He won't look at me. This is good. It means I'm winning. I have to admit, it's nice to see him sweat things. I pull the cord, turning off the warm glow of the open sign and then click the lock on the door. He resumes his pacing. "Just tell me what was going through your head to make you do something so stupid?"

He's like a lion in a cage. Caught. Trying to find his way out. "I-I…"

He stops abruptly. His hands go to his hips. Finally, his eyes meet mine. "You what?"

"I hadn't heard from you in almost a week. I was desperate to see you." *Love is sweet misery, and you see Grant, I can play too.*

He looks exasperated by my answer. He's just realized I'm a loose cannon, and he's trying to figure out how to reign me in. He doesn't know it, but deep down this is the part he enjoys the most. He likes losing control even if it's what he fears most. "So you thought going to my home would be a way for us to spend quality time together?"

My eyebrow rises. "No—"

"You know my situation Isobel," he tells me. There's a hint of warning in his tone, a hard edge. He's playing daddy, and I like it. "You know I'm married... and you know my family is the most important thing in the world to me."

Ouch. That stings. I stare at the tiles on the floor. *You will not put me in my place, Grant Dunn. Unless my place is with you.*

Still, bile creeps up the back of my throat, and it tastes like regret. I knew I shouldn't have gone. I thought it would give me insight as to how to get closer to him, to better understand his life. But I can see now it's only done the opposite. I hadn't given a lot of thought as to how he might react, and honestly, I sort of expected he would be happy to see me. I thought it would make things wild and dangerous. I thought it would add fuel to the fire. On the plus side, he's here.

And yet...it had the opposite effect. I know what he's about to say but that doesn't make it hurt any less when it comes.

"I think we're going to have to stop seeing each other."

"Grant—look—" I have to stop myself. Jesus. He's being melodramatic. I exhale long and slow. What comes next will be more meaningful that way. "I'm sorry...."

"My wife is asking all sorts of questions. Do you have any idea how hard it is to hide an affair when it's out in the open?"

I fold my arms over my chest. "Sounds like you have experience."

He eyes me from head to toe, evaluating me in his meticulous way. Finally, he softens a bit. I can tell by the way the corner of his eyes relax. The crow's feet thin out. He looks around at the mess the teenagers left in their wake. Trash, wadded up napkins, empty cups. "Are you almost done here?"

"Yes," I say, although I have at least an hour's worth of work to do to get the place in shape for the morning shift. Screw it. I'll just come in early.

"Good." He glances around once more. "Because we need to talk, and I'd rather not do it here."

~

IT'S FREEZING OUT. HE CRANKS UP THE HEATER UNTIL IT'S STIFLING, almost unbearable, and then we drive. We take the same route we took only weeks ago now. The vibe is different this time. It's not carefree and hopeful. It's somber and unrelenting. My heart pounds. *This is it,* I tell myself. *This was your problem from the get-go; you got too used to a good thing and now look what you've done.*

He pulls off the highway and takes a feeder road. We drive forever. Finally, just when I think we'll never stop, he pulls over. He doesn't kill the engine, he simply puts the car in park and stares straight ahead.

"Look," I say trying to remedy the silence. I want to fill the space. I want to close the gap I've caused between us. "I'm sorry. But I can fix this."

He cocks his head and studies my face. "How do you plan to do that?"

"I don't know. But I will."

"My wife suspects an affair, Isobel. I'm afraid this thing we have," he motions between us, "is going to have to end."

"But it doesn't," I plead. "She doesn't know for sure. We just have to be more careful is all."

He shakes his head slowly. "She will take everything, you know. The house, the kids, my practice, she'll get it all."

"She can't take your work from you."

"She is entitled to half of everything," he assures me. "She can, and she will. Combine that with the support I'll have to pay her for the kids and well...I might as well pack it in."

I don't know what to say, except I've heard it all before.

He checks his phone. "I saw it happen to our friend Tom. He nearly lost everything."

"But you aren't Tom."

He almost smiles. "You're so young," he says, trailing his finger down my face. "You really have no idea how nasty divorces can be do you?"

He knows I don't. My husband is dead. I shake my head.

"I'm in love with you, Isobel. But I can't lose everything."

"Then don't."

This sets him off. He throws up his hands. He wants me to concede, to tell him I understand. He wants me to make it easy for him. He doesn't know me. "What am I supposed to do?"

I mimic his shrug. "Be with me."

"It's not that simple."

"Nothing is." He appreciates the truth.

"I need to know I can trust you."

I don't know what he wants from me. *He loves me. He loves me not.* "Of course, you can."

"Do you want children Isobel?"

"I don't know," I say. My voice comes out shrill. I hate the way it gives me away when I lie. "I haven't given it much thought…"

"I need you to," he tells me earnestly. "I also need you to think about how far you're willing to go for love—for us."

"I think if we just talk to her—if we just tell her the truth—she'll understand. It's not like we meant for this to happen."

"You don't know Josie."

I don't know what he means by this. But I know enough to know she has a lifestyle I'd want to hang onto if I were in her shoes. Literally.

"She'll never let me go that easy." He presses his lips together. "She'll never let me off the hook."

"What do we do?"

He doesn't answer immediately. I can see the wheels turning. "You leave that to me," he says when I reach for his hand. He doesn't pull away. "For now— I want to make love to you one last time."

I climb in the backseat. He follows. He's soft and tender and desperate and so full of shit.

I cry afterward. It takes a lot. But I manage. "This can't be our last time."

Grant wipes the tears from my eyes. "Then let's do something crazy."

"Like run away together?" I ask buttoning my jeans. I realize afterward how stupid this sounds and I wish I could take it back.

He shakes his head. "No," he says. "Something else."

I raise my brow and wait for him to tell me more. "Can I trust you Isobel?"

"I told you, you could," I scoff. This is getting annoying. I hate needy men. "I've said it a million times."

He narrows his gaze. "Good," he says. "Now, I'm going to have to ask you to prove it to me."

CHAPTER TWENTY-SEVEN

JOSIE

"I'd like an Americano, please," I say. I stumble on the last word. She doesn't deserve niceties. Old habits die hard. She nods in confirmation and I can see in her expression, she knows I know. How strange to know that someone you're so close to can have a life without you. I wonder what he's told her about me. I shouldn't wonder these things. At this point, it's futile.

"How long have you been sleeping with my husband?" I ask. She knows the answer, of course. I can see by the way she chews at her lip. I'd be willing to bet she knows right down to the minute. Grant has that way about him. Even now, even after everything, I still get it. *Five weeks, three days, and two hours? Longer?*

Finally, she shrugs. She's not very good at being direct. I bet my husband likes that.

I study her carefully, wondering what else he likes that I've missed. "You don't think I deserve the dignity of an answer?"

This time she doesn't just chew at her lip. She bites. Hard. It starts to bleed a little. She licks it away. "A few weeks."

She hands me my coffee. "Can we talk?" I ask motioning toward a table.

"We're kind of busy," she says.

"Not that busy." I made sure to come at the appropriate time. I didn't want to be completely alone. But I didn't want her to be too swamped, either.

She shrugs again. "Okay." She goes into the back and returns with an older woman. The two of them speak briefly. I watch as the older woman takes over, and then I take a seat at an empty table in the corner. I wonder how many times Grant has been here. Did he tell her about the sandwich incident? Did they have a good laugh at my expense? Was it his way of making sure there was enough distance between his mistress and myself or was it just his usual shenanigans? I don't know. Maybe I never will.

Izzy slides the chair out from the table and drags it across the floor. She wants me to think she's doing me a favor.

I don't waste any time. I've done enough of that. "My husband isn't the man you think he is," I pause to blow on my coffee. "But then, I don't know what you think. I can only guess."

She glances down at the table. She folds her hands and puts them in her lap. She unfolds them and rubs her palms on her knees. She's fidgeting. But also bracing herself. She expects me to be angry, probably even to hurl my coffee in her face. I surprise her when I offer a smile instead.

"I know it's wrong—I know what I've—what *we've* done is wrong. But we didn't mean—"

Guilt is a powerful thing.

"I love him—" She just puts it out there just like that.

"Don't—" I say, cutting her off. I place my coffee on the table. "Like I said. You don't know him."

She tilts her head. She wants a challenge, when she's already entered the ring. "I know enough."

I don't respond. Not at first. I wait until she doesn't think I'm going to. Meanwhile, I nurse my Americano and stare out the window. I could cry. But I won't. Still, even dry-eyed, I need to make it uncomfortable for her. It's the least I can do seeing the way she's made my life suddenly uninhabitable.

I watch people outside coming and going. People oblivious to the fact that while they're nonchalantly going about their simple business, I'm in here dealing with the worst kind. Betrayal. It's hard to see it coming. Not because you trust the other person. But because you so desperately wanted to. I think about how Grant and I stopped here after seeing June. It seems like a lifetime ago. In reality it wasn't. I think about posting a shot of my coffee on Instalook: *It all started with an Americano.* Or: *Coffee with my husband's mistress. It's a new day.*

Instead, I turn and meet her gaze. "I was like you once," I confess. "Naive. Hopeful. A fool."

She furrows her brow. "I'm not that green."

I can't help myself. I choke on nothing. Or maybe it's not nothing. Maybe it's the bitterness that's been there all along creeping toward the surface. "No?" I hear myself say. "What did you think? That my husband is going to leave me for you?" I motion around the place. "For what? For a waitress in a coffee shop only slightly older than his own daughter?"

"He wants to be with me, Josie." She says it matter of factly. Like it's either true or she's rehearsed it. Either way, my name sounds strange coming from her lips. Her eyes flicker. She looks like she wants to crawl under the table. Like she wants to hide, like she's just spoken a secret into existence and has just realized she can't reel it back. She drops her voice to match her eyes. "He's scared, though," she continues. "He's afraid of you."

My eyes grow wide. "Did Grant tell you this himself? Or is it another of your childish inferences?"

"No. I mean yes." She backtracks. "He said you'd take everything."

I laugh and it isn't the laugh of a woman who has it all together. It's maniacal, animalistic. "If you believe that—then I was right. You don't know my husband at all."

THERE'S A DIFFERENCE IN THINKING OF DOING SOMETHING TERRIBLE and actually doing it. But as it turns out, it's a very thin line indeed. What I'm still in the process of deciding is at which point you go from one side to the other. Is it possible to cross it before you realize? At which point can you still turn back?

I should have known coming to this side of town would be trouble. Of course, my husband should've known, too. He told me he had to work late. That's what they always say. Now—not only do I have a deceptive husband— I have a gun on my hands. A gun I won't know how to explain.

There are lots of scenarios in life that have rules. Playbooks. Like if this happens, you do that. If X, then Y and Z. But where's the playbook for having a philandering husband and a loaded gun that isn't yours? If I call the cops and tell them I was just almost robbed at gunpoint, then what? That's the problem these days. Everyone's trying to take what's not theirs to take. Surely, they will want a statement. They will want to know why I was here. If I explain that I wanted to see them together, that I had to see it for myself, will they think I'm crazy? A scorned wife looking for attention? Because I have to be honest, that's what I would think.

On the other hand, if they give me the benefit of the doubt, will they take me downtown for questioning? Will there be line-ups? I have a lot on my plate right now and that sounds time consuming. Somehow I don't think telling the cops I'm not sure how I'll fit it all in is going to fly. Alternatively, what will I say to my husband when he realizes I was spying on him? What will I say when everyone wants to know why I was on this side of town? People want details. That's the best part of any story. Certainly, it would be the punch line in this one.

My husband would know what to say. I'm not as good a liar as he is. That's why I'm in this mess.

I text my husband. 'Have you eaten?'

Of course, he's eaten.

He texts back almost immediately. This confirms my suspicion. Whatever he feels for her, it's more than just sex. Otherwise, he'd be in and out. My husband's profession has trained him for this. Every minute spent is a dollar wasted somewhere else.

I read his response: Swamped here with charts. I'll pick something up.

Chlamydia. Gonorrhea. Herpes. A bastard child. I turn the gun over in my hands. It's heavier than I thought it would be. I reach over into the passenger seat and use my scarf to wipe my prints. I have no idea if this even works. I've seen it in the movies.

What are you going to do, Josie? Make your move. If this were a game of chess, and isn't all of life, then I'd have to be patient. Chess matches are usually won via a mixture of patience and the ability to predict your opponent's next move.

I need to know my husband's next move. That's why I came. But now that I'm here, I'm not sure I want to know. I picture the two of them together. I think of her in our home. A protective instinct ignites inside me.

My mind flashes to the lilies in the coffee shop. I could be sick. *You're a fool. Everyone knew. Everyone but you.* Something in me shifts. I've covered up bruises for years. Bruises are easy to conceal. Another woman, this kind of betrayal, is different. It can't be hidden with a little makeup. I will not be made a fool of. *I have a decision to make.*

Just then something shifts in my periphery. My husband comes bounding down the stairs. He isn't supposed to look happy. But he does. He's supposed to look paranoid, guilty, if nothing else. He's light on his feet. I wonder if he's making up his lie with each step toward our side of town. Or if he has it down already. I wonder what he'll say when he sees my face. I wonder if he'll pick a fight. Ask me to step on the scale. I wonder what offense he'll come up with this time in order to shift the focus from his own transgressions. I wonder how many times he's asked me for a blow job when he's already been inside her. I pick up the gun, wrap it in my scarf and stuff it in my purse. It's not like I can just dump it. That would be irresponsible. Plus, it's nice to have a secret of my own.

CHAPTER TWENTY-EIGHT

IZZY

"Relax," Tyler tells me. He plops down on my couch and lets his head rest against the wall. Eventually, his eyes fall to half-mast. "You're too wound up."

I walk the length of my small apartment and back again. "How could this happen?"

"Like I told you—" His eyes are all the way closed.

"Just tell me again you're sure she didn't see your face."

He sits up and pulls his pipe from his jacket pocket. I watch as he lights it up. He takes a hit and then meets my gaze directly. "You need to chill."

I scroll through Instalook. She hasn't posted today. I feel sick.

"Relax," he tells me again. He takes another hit. I stare at my phone, rereading Grant's texts. Sometimes I just like to see his name on the screen. I want to text him now but I'm afraid. It would be an admission of my failure, and I'm not ready to concede. An image of his face in my bed flickers in my mind.

Tyler brushes his palms across his thighs like he's just getting warmed up. He places his pipe on the coffee table and relaxes into my couch. I want to punch him. "She didn't see my face."

I should have known better than to ask him. I really should

have. "Jesus. Tyler," I exhale loudly. "I told you there was a lot riding on this."

He motions toward the pipe and then kicks his feet up. I won't smoke dope at a time like this. Something horrible has happened, and I feel justifiably terrible.

"But I don't know, Iz." His mouth stretches into a thin line. "That bitch...the way she took the gun...I'd be careful if I were you. She seems a bit off her rocker."

I perch on the edge of the couch. "I still don't understand how she got the gun."

"You told me not to kill her." He throws his hands in the air. His tone is not apologetic. "You said you just wanted me to scare her." He gestures widely. "What was I supposed to do? Tackle her for it?"

"I don't know," I admit. "This is a nightmare."

He cocks his head. "Where's my money? I'm going to eat now that I'm going to have to buy Big Sean a new piece."

"Big Sean? Seriously? What kind of name is that?" Suddenly, I get the urge to get high. I need something to take the edge off.

He shrugs. "He's a big guy—one that I'm going to have to buy a new gun— otherwise it'll be me who ends up swimming with the fishes."

I roll my eyes. "Maybe I should've just gotten Big Sean to do the job."

He looks away dismissing me. "What was she doing around your place anyway? That's not how it was supposed to go down."

"I don't know. Her husband was here, I guess she followed."

Tyler stands. He's getting antsy. He's probably going to ask for a fuck. "See— like I said— crazy— now where is my money?"

"Don't worry, you'll get your money."

"You don't have it, do you?"

"He doesn't want to pay people for a job that's not done. What can I say?"

His look suggests he thinks I'm lying. "Here's what you can say

— you tell that motherfucker his wife is crazy— and if he isn't careful and he doesn't get me my money, I might just tell her what he's up to."

"You know, Tyler, you really don't know me very well. You should be careful about empty threats."

His narrowed eyes open. "Who said it's empty?"

"Get out," I say pointing at the door. "I'll have your money for you tomorrow."

"I hope so," he says. I feel nothing. He puffs his cheeks and exhales. "You should be careful. And not just with the crazy wife. Funny thing about that, Izzy. You don't know me as well as you think you do. I'm not exactly the kind of guy that lets himself just get fucked over."

～

TYLER LEAVES HIS PIPE. I SEARCH THE KITCHEN FOR A LIGHTER, SIT down, and take a few hits. I relax into myself. I consider taking the half-empty bottle I stuffed under the kitchen counter for occasions such as this but I check Instalook to buy time. Really, I need to talk to Grant, and I don't want to be hammered when he calls. I run through my story again. I want to have my facts straight when he calls.

Okay, sure. He wasn't supposed to let her get the gun. But Tyler is a pussy.

I take a third hit. The smoke settles in my lungs. The tension leaves my body.

We were supposed to scare her. He did at least accomplish that.

I check Instalook again. Still nothing.

Grant should have called by now. Why hasn't he called? Maybe Josie has gone to the police. Maybe she's told them about me. Maybe she's forcing him to console her.

Thoughts race through my mind. Pot doesn't usually make me

this paranoid. Grant should have called. He must be pissed at me. He probably wants to end things. Seeing how distraught Josie had to have been, he's realized how much he loves her. I'm going to be alone forever. *Fuck it. He isn't going to call. Might as well.* I go for the vodka. I unscrew the cap and fill a shot glass. I won't use a chaser. I deserve to feel the burn.

This is not the way it was supposed to happen.

I'M ITCHING ALL OVER. SOMETHING IS WRONG. I TEXT TYLER AND ask him what kind of weed that was. He texts back: Sucker. Then a smiley face emoji.

I don't know what this means. My head is swimming. I rub at my eyes. It doesn't fix the blurriness.

I stand and go into the bathroom. I splash water on my face. It helps. At least now, I can see things. Things like a nearly empty vodka bottle sitting beside Tyler's pipe. *Surely, I didn't drink all of that.* No, I would remember.

My palms are sweaty. My heart races. I'm burning up.

I need to eat something. I need to sober up. I have no idea how much time has passed. Everything seems slow. I check the time on my phone. There's a text from Grant: We need to talk. Can you come over?

Shit. I was wrong. He does want me. There's no time to sober up. I have to go now. I walk two doors down to Tyler's apartment and bang on the door. He opens it slowly and then leans against the doorframe. Inside, I see people strewn about the place. Music is blaring. A guy playing video games turns and glances over his shoulder. He says something to the guy next to him. They both laugh and turn back to their game. Tyler eyes me from head to toe and then runs his hands through his hair.

"Jesus, Izzy."

"I need your keys."

He shakes his head from side to side. Very slowly. "Not a chance in hell."

"You fucking drugged me."

His brow forms a V. "I'm not giving you my keys."

He doesn't deny it. He doesn't have to.

"You're drunk, Izzy," he tells me. He can't know that. Vodka doesn't smell.

"What is it?" I demand. I feel faint. I feel my pulse in my ears. It could be the music. "What did you give me?"

"Nothing. Go home and sleep it off," he tells me. Then he laughs and swings his door wide open. "Or better yet, come inside."

I stand on my tippy-toes and point my finger in his face. "I will fucking murder you."

"Whoa," he says, holding his palms up. Everyone is watching now. I know what they're thinking. Lover's quarrel. But Tyler is not my lover. Their eyes make me angry. "I HATE YOU," I scream. I direct all of my bitterness at him. It's real, too. This is his fault. Grant is supposed to be with me. He fucked up. Now I'm alone. Now I'll always be alone. I momentarily forget my mission. I forget Grant's text. I'm fueled by anger.

Tyler sighs long and slow. "It was just a little PCP."

"PCP? Why?" I close my eyes. I feel myself sway. I might cry. I hate myself. I feel him grip my forearm. "It's just a bump. It wasn't for you. It was for me. Anyway, I didn't think you'd smoke it. And I sure as shit didn't think you'd get wasted and...get high...you never smoke anymore..." I don't open my eyes when he speaks. He drags me down the hall. I half go willingly, half drag my feet.

"I hate you Tyler. I FUCKING HATE YOU."

"Someone's had a long day," he says mockingly. "Off to bed you go."

"I don't neeeeed to go to bed." I can hear the slur in my speech. "Grant loves me. He wants ME. I have to go there."

"Trust me, you don't want lover boy to see you like this. He's not that kind of guy."

I feel rage. Burning hot rage. "You don't know what kind of guy he is!"

His grip tightens. It hurts. I jerk away. He lets me go. "I know he's married like the last one."

My heart sinks. "Josh."

"Yeah, Izzy. Josh. Josh isn't dead."

I swallow hard. He's knocked the wind out of me. I sink to the floor.

He eyes me with pity and a bit of something else. "I don't know why you lied," he says quietly. "And quite frankly, I don't care. But you need help."

CHAPTER TWENTY-NINE

JOSIE

Physical pain you can block out. Emotional pain is harder to drown. It always finds its way to the surface. I feel the needle tear through my scalp. *One stitch, two stitches. Three.* I wince. I shouldn't have acted like nothing happened. I should have told him the truth. I forgot the details. Grant always remembers details.

"Oh, stop being a baby," he says, pulling. "I numbed you up."

I think it's just another of his lies. I feel every tug, every pinch. I feel everything. I stuff it down.

"Why wouldn't you listen, Josie? Why do you have to make everything hard?"

The gun sits on the table. He found it. First, the text on his phone. Before that, the location log on mine.

"Why did you bring her into this?"

"I wanted answers." Also, I knew she would come. I wanted her to come. I don't tell him this though.

"After everything I've done for you... after everything I've done for this family. For the church, for my career. Everything. And look at you. You insist on making a mockery of me. You want

BRITNEY KING

to make *me* the bad guy. That was June's problem, too. She was always so nosy, always sticking her head where it didn't belong."

Relax. If he were going to kill me, he certainly wouldn't go through the trouble of stitching me up.

I feel myself going under. I'm slipping back into the darkness. I refuse to fight it.

"You had it so good, Josie. The clothes, the house, the kids. And what did I ever ask of you? To have sex with me when I wanted it? To look nice? To do a bit of manual labor when the going got tough. Was that really so much to ask?"

I want to tell him that he's abused me for years. I want to tell him that he won't win this. Not even if he kills me. But who am I kidding? He's already won. He won't kill me. He likes to see me suffer.

The doorbell chimes then, bringing me back from the darkness.

"Oh, good," he says slipping the last of the stitching through. I feel him tie it off. His tone is smooth and sarcastic. "Stay here. Our little guest is back."

"JUST LET ME TALK TO HER," SHE SAYS. HER VOICE COMES OUT garbled. I think I have a concussion. My brain is fuzzy. Like her words. "I'll make her understand."

"Isobel—please." He's trying to calm her. He hasn't yet resorted to using his hands to silence her. "Just listen. It was a mistake, you coming here. Josie is very upset, and she's gone to bed. I told you that the first time."

More garbled speech.

I strain to hear. My husband's voice is clear. It's survival that lets me hear. "If you hang on a minute, I'll get my keys and drive you home."

I can't hear nor understand what she says. Grant is looking for his keys. I can hear that. I recall him throwing them earlier. He's hidden mine. I won't be driving for a while. Not with a concussion and not after he realized I followed him. Instalook has gone by the way of my cell phone. I used our family plan to text her from his number. I wanted her to come.

I force myself to stand and open the door. I want her to know he's a liar. I don't want that text to have been sent in vain. I also want him to leave without locking me in. He does that sometimes. He knows I won't run. I've made that mistake before. But only once.

If he's going to kill me, better to have a witness. Plus, I invited her here for a reason. She needs to see what she's caused. She needs to know what she's walking into.

I round the corner. She gasps. "Oh my God."

I don't know how my face looks. But I'm guessing not good.

"He'll do this to you, too," I say.

"Come on, Josie. Don't scare the girl." Grant laughs nervously. "My wife was attacked today."

I don't say anything. I watch her face. She believes him. Also, it's apparent she's drunk.

He looks at me before turning to her. "Would you mind waiting outside?"

My stomach turns when she nods and heads toward the front door.

I vomit on myself when I hear it open and close.

"What in the fuck, Josie? Now—not only will she not leave me alone, she'll talk. She'll have something to use against us."

"She's not stalking you, Grant. You're having an affair. There's a difference."

"You see, that's where you're wrong. I want nothing to do with her. She has dozens of photos of you, of our entire family, on her phone. I tried to tell you." He backhands me. "You never listen."

"Why can't you listen?" I taste blood.

"Grant." This time he goes for my hair. He wants to put a stop to any scene I might cause. He wants to shut me up.

I smell it before I realize what's happened. Of course, I see it, it happens in slow motion, although it happens fast. Gunpowder fills my nose. Then blood, but the fear came first. I thought it was mine. But it wasn't mine alone. Now, I hear nothing but screams.

"Oh my God! No. No. Noooooo." She screams and she screams and she screams. "I didn't mean—"

CHAPTER THIRTY

IZZY

I only wanted to return the gun to Tyler. Mostly, I didn't want to have to cough up the money to "Big Sean." I didn't have it to cough up. That's why I picked it up. That I remember, that much I'm sure of. The rest is a bit hazy. It will come later, I'm sure of it. I shouldn't have gone there. I should have waited outside. I shouldn't have been so nosey.

I don't remember pulling the trigger. I don't remember much of what happened afterward. What I do remember is her face. I remember Grant's lifeless body lying on the floor.

"Now look what you've done." I remember she said that.

I remember the way he looked, lying there. Aside from all the blood, the pained expression, and wide-eyed stare, he could have just been sleeping. I don't think I ever saw him sleep, come to think of it. So I told myself it could have been true.

I don't even remember the screaming. I don't remember my admission of guilt. They tell me it was all there in the screams. They told me I said at the scene of the crime, I didn't mean to do it. I didn't.

Yet, Grant Dunn is dead.

And they say it's my fault.

CHAPTER THIRTY-ONE

JOSIE

It started with a white lie. I guess you could say I learned from the best. It was easy really. They wanted a certain story; I let them lead the witness.

"I know you're tired Mrs. Dunn," the detective tells me. Classic projection. "Forgive me," he says glancing at my statement. "I just want to make sure we have this straight."

I stare at the cold, hard metal table. You always read about these kinds of rooms in police stations. You never realize the descriptions are quite so accurate. "So—just to get the timeline straight. Your husband texts Izzy Lewis and says he needs to speak to her. This occurs at approximately 7:02 p.m." He proceeds to go through the events once again. This is the third time. Please let it be the charm. I twist my wedding rings and nod. I do not look at him. My tears fall against the table. I feel something soft graze my arm. I look up. Tissues.

"Yes," I say. "I mean, I didn't see the text. But I assume that's right." I make a point to be careful in my admissions.

He rattles on listing out the details. "And before Ms. Lewis fired the weapon, can you tell me what she said."

"She didn't say anything."

"And the deceased—I'm sorry—your husband," he pauses, he looks genuinely sorry. "What did he say?"

"He said that he wasn't having an affair. That Ms. Lewis was stalking him. That she wouldn't leave him alone."

"Do you think that Ms. Lewis was, in fact, stalking him? Had he mentioned it?"

I start crying.

"Had she shown up at your home before?" I think of the two of them in our kitchen. I think of her with our daughter.

"Yes." I cry some more.

He nods as though he expected me to say this. "Ms. Lewis has a history of stalking, I'm afraid."

I place my face in my hands and rub.

"How did she seem when she showed up?"

He wants to know if she came there to murder my husband. I've seen enough television.

"Drunk."

"Well, we'll know about that soon enough."

"Did she seem angry?"

"She refused to leave."

"Earlier in the evening a similar incident occurred with a neighbor of hers. She threatened to murder him."

My eyes grow wide. Sometimes you get lucky. Me, I am the luckiest. I hit the jackpot.

I HAVE TO EXPLAIN TO MY CHILDREN THEIR FATHER'S MURDER. THIS in and of itself is bad enough. Do I want them to know the kind of man their father was? Not really. Why inflict that kind of pain on them if I don't have to? So far, they know their dad made a mistake. A chance encounter in a coffee shop led to us being stalked and ultimately to him making a bad decision. He had an affair. That part is clear. Izzy Lewis has a history of stalking married men. So when I met her at Lucky's, and I saw the way she looked at my husband, it made her an easy target. I hadn't thought her pretty enough to get him to stray. I only hoped. A bit of digging, and I found out she had charges filed against her. I knew the hand my husband would play. I knew he was tracking my every move. I knew if I visited Lucky's again, he would, too. He saw the way the girl acted. She was perfect for New Hope. Young, gullible and lonely. Easy prey. The worker bee type.

What can I say? I wanted out. I didn't care if she took my husband, not at first. Not until I saw the way people pitied June. Not until I saw another woman fitted into her life like the final missing piece of a jigsaw puzzle now solved. I didn't want that for my children. Grant didn't deserve a clean slate. Also, I couldn't be certain I wouldn't end up like June.

So I lied. I lied and I lied, and I kept on lying. I didn't want to admit Grant was abusive. That he wanted out. I didn't want to admit Izzy Lewis acted in self-defense, that she was trying to save my life. I could have told the truth about why Izzy shot my husband and why. But what's the point? She was hell-bent on destroying my family, whether or not I wanted it destroyed. She dug her own grave, stalking me on Instalook. Later, during the trial, I would learn, it was in fact her who sent me pictures of shellfish and got my daughter expelled from school. She hired her friend to rob and rough me up. Those things were on her. She had to pay for her mistakes. Everyone does. It's not my fault a jury of her peers sentenced her to death. How am I to know she wasn't going to shoot me that night? Who's to say? It's not like she can be trusted. She proved that when she slept with a married man. And a dozen times since.

Facts are facts. And the fact is, my husband is dead, and everyone loves a good story.

It's not all bad, though. I got out from under the church, turns out they're the only ones who don't want a good scandal on their hands. Although, that will come soon enough, I'm sure. There's something to be said about a woman scorned. I think of June and her missed opportunity. I could have turned out like that. Me, I have a reputation to protect. People can take a lot from you, I have learned. Your husband, your wealth, even your life. But your reputation, you must never let them take that.

So, no, I don't feel sorry for Izzy Lewis. I don't feel sorry for my husband. Their mistakes should serve as a warning to every person out there considering an affair. Be careful who you get tangled up with...you just never know.

CHAPTER THIRTY-TWO

IZZY

Mountain View Prison Unit, Gatesville, Texas

R ight out of the gate, there's something you should know. I am not a good person. So don't go feeling sorry for me. If anything, let my story serve as a cautionary tale. Love is blind. That you should remember. As for the rest, well, it's complex, and quite frankly, a jury of my peers have already made their decision.

As it turns out, whether it was the right one is irrelevant once it's been made. This is what I'm guilty of: I searched these people out. I wanted in, and in that respect I got what I wanted. It just so happened to be more than I bargained for. Real life doesn't work like it does on television. If a crime is committed, someone has to pay. And the law, as much as we'd like to believe, isn't that black and white. Add the fact that you have real people, fallible people, with their own experiences, judgments, and beliefs they bring to the table, judging your fate, and well, it's not as simple as they want you to believe. Less so, when you're 'the other woman' with a long history of making bad decisions. In that case, you'd better be prepared to pay when your number is called.

"Inmate," I hear the guard say. His voice is deep, thick with false bravado. Still, I flinch when I hear my number called, even after all this time. "Let's get a move on. They ain't gonna wait all day."

Stalling, I stare at the clothes that were delivered to me. I don't want to disturb them; they're almost too pretty to touch. *Play with fire, get burned,* I hear my mother say. *A woman should be reserved in all things.* I remember Grant saying that once. This has always been my problem. I never set out to be a troublemaker, quite the opposite actually. It's just I never could resist doing something I wasn't supposed to do.

Running my fingers over the soft material, I feel the hurt bubble up, and I do my best to stuff it back down into its rightful place. You have to do that in here. *If only you'd been better at doing it on the outside.* It's just that it's been so long since I've felt something this nice, this soft, this real. It's just a blouse and a pencil skirt, a little reminder from the old days, but it feels like I've won. Small victories. Sometimes that's all a person can ask for.

I wonder if they'll let me keep them when this is all said and done. Probably not. I make a mental note to ask— it's little things like this that keep you sane, that remind you that you're still alive. In the end, I probably won't ask after all. *Stupid questions get stupid answers.*

I check the tags; they're new, a condition of the terms I agreed to in exchange for the interview. It's nice to have a bit of leverage, and nice clothes was one of my requests. For this, in the off chance that she might be watching, I want to be seen in something other than bright orange scrubs. I want to be seen as human. I don't know if that's still a possibility. Once you're in here, it's easy to be forgotten. Thankfully, I have something they want. Something that sells. That something is a story.

Here's what they want to know: Had I known I was going to be sentenced to die for my crimes, would I have done things differently?

It's probably the one question that matters more than

anything. Even now, I'm not sure how I'll answer. It's a tough question, and while I have a lot of time on my hands to mull it over, I'd propose that it's not that simple. What I want to say is this: The reality of who someone is online and the reality of who that person is in real life are often two different things. When it comes to saving their own ass, people will always turn on you. Friends. Lovers. Everyone. Remember that.

This makes me think of Tyler. He got off easy. He didn't admit to the drugs in my system being his. He didn't admit to the gun I used coming from anyone named 'Big Sean.' He said I made it all up. What he did admit to was witnessing me stalk the Dunns online. Two lies, one truth.

Everyone knows drug users are unreliable.

The guard bangs on the door with his fist. "Coming," I say and I deftly slip the orange prison uniform shirt over my head. It's stamped with Death Row Unit in big black letters as though I could forget. I unclasp the granny bra and slide the new one on. I check myself in the small plastic mirror and I smile. You can't imagine what a good fitting bra will do for one's self-esteem. In here, everything is issued, everything is mostly the same. Nothing is my own anymore. I've been reduced to having basic necessities dished out to me as though I'm an animal, caged and on display.

She thinks she's better than us, I hear them say as I'm escorted down the corridor. I know there will be hell to pay for this later, but I might as well enjoy it now. This is probably the last time I'll wear plain clothes, the last time I'll remember what it felt like to look like a woman, the last time anyone will be jealous of me. And even after all this time, even knowing I'm going to die, I still want what I've always wanted: envy.

I've been offered good money to give this interview, to tell my side of the story, and I can only assume this comes with being one of only seven women on death row in the entirety of the United States.

This is my third attempt at this interview and judging by the way the last two went, I bet they're thinking what I'm thinking. Hopefully the third time will be the charm. I'm led to a chair in the center of the room. My hands are cuffed, but they assure me I'll be filmed from the waist up. The woman interviewing me has already taken her place. I study her as she stares at her phone. She's pretty, in a plain sort of way. I watch as she crosses and uncrosses her legs, and I wonder what she could possibly have to be nervous about. Already I have forgotten what life on the outside is like. I forget that it's also a dog-eat-dog world out there, maybe even more so than in here, because at least in this place we are governed by rules. I feel sweat bead up at my temples. It could be nerves or it could be the bright lights overhead. Someone dusts powder across my nose. There's a flurry of activity around, a buzz about the place I haven't felt in a long time.

The woman looks up. "Ready?" she asks offering a reassuring smile.

I nod slightly. I can see that she thinks I'm going to run again. She leans forward a little, lowers her gaze and then her voice. "Just remember why you're doing this."

"Oh, you mean for the freedom?"

She laughs nervously. She doesn't understand my sarcasm. Although, whether she gets me matters not. We both know I've exhausted my appeals. That's why the price tag on the interview went up. Time isn't on my side. "There's freedom in telling your story, you know," she offers sympathetically.

I want to tell her she's wrong about that. Telling my story will change nothing. I'm not doing this for me. I'm doing it for her. I've thought about what I might want to say to her. And mostly, I want to say I'm sorry. I want to let her know that it's okay. I own up to my part in all of this. Unlike her, I wasn't given much of a choice. So, I'm not without blame. Still, it's high time she owns up to the part she played. I want to hear her say it. Words have power. In here, they're the only power.

"People are very curious about you," the producer tells me as they affix a mic to the underside of my collar. She's holding a cup off coffee, I watch the steam eke out from the small slit in the lid. It makes me think of Americanos, and it's funny how things seem to have a way of finding their way around, out, and through. The smell makes my stomach audibly growl. God, it's been so long. She takes a sip and then swallows like it gives her life. "They all want to hear what you have to say."

"They want to know what I'm doing with the money," I reply with the tilt of my head. That's what she thinks, too. I can see it in the whites of her eyes. And why wouldn't she think that? Everything she does is for the money. Otherwise, why would she waste such a lovely day in a maximum security prison?

She laughs. "Yes, probably." I don't tell her that the money has nothing to do with it. After all, what good will money do me in here?

"Just relax and answer the questions truthfully," she adds with a smile. "Shouldn't take too long." *What reason do I have to lie?* When you're on death row, honesty isn't a virtue people see when they look at you. They want to know if the things they say about me are true. They want to hear it from the horse's mouth, even if they won't believe it.

But what is truth? Whose truth do they want? Mine? Hers? Mostly, they want to hear that you're remorseful.

Am I sorry? I'd like to think the answer would be yes—that if I'd known, I would have made different choices. But there isn't room for maybes. It's absolutes they seek. They want confirmation that the choice I made was the wrong one. It isn't a martyr they want. Dying for my sins is not enough for them. They want to be able to rest their heads easily with the notion I know what I did was wrong. Modern society runs on the idea that I'm supposed to feel remorse.

But that's the one thing I have left in my control: the way I feel. Everything else has been taken from me, so forgive me, but I think maybe I'll hold on to this one last thing.

On the other hand, if truth is what they're seeking, the truth is yes, it was love. No matter the outcome, I loved him. And if one has to die...what greater cause is there than love?

That's not to say I didn't know the odds. I'm not a simpleton. I know there are approximately 6.5 billion people on the planet, and sure, I could have loved any one of them. I could have made different choices. But I didn't.

The anchor starts to speak; we're going live any moment. However, I'm not here. I'm somewhere else. It's not the interviewer's voice I hear. It's someone else's.

I'm picturing her face, and I'm wondering if I ever cross her mind. I guess that's what we're all seeking. To be remembered. This need alone makes me certain, if not hopeful, that my name has run through her mind, at least momentarily. Surely, you can't just erase a person that easily, like chalk on a chalkboard, like they were nothing. It wasn't nothing, what happened. I have to believe that. Otherwise, I'd go crazy. Perhaps that's the unfairness of it all, was simply that her poker face was better. That's why I'm in here while she's out there.

They're going to ask me about her. About how much I knew. Other things, too. I haven't quite worked out what I'll say. She knows what she's done. To let everyone in on her trickery is unnecessary. But to say it wouldn't give me a certain satisfaction to know she's thinking of me would be a lie. I hope it hurts, too. I hope my name runs through her mind on a path of destruction like nothing she's seen. I hope the memories strike with a jagged edge. I hope they cut deep. For she deserves nothing less than searing, burning, white-hot pain.

They're counting down now. *Here goes nothing.* This is where they make an example out of me. *Look, look at what can happen. Can you imagine?*

It's pretty amazing if you think about it—and I have plenty of time for that—how they say one bad choice leads to another bad choice and then onto another, until eventually you're sitting, waiting to die, and wondering whether it'll come soon. Sometimes, I think about what it will be like when it does. *Will she come? Will she say goodbye? Will she apologize?* Perhaps that is the worst of it all. The punishment isn't that they're going to kill me. But that I have to wait to find out.

A NOTE FROM BRITNEY

Dear Reader,

I hope you enjoyed reading *The Social Affair*. If you have a moment and you'd like to let me know what you thought, feel free to drop me an email. I enjoy hearing from readers.

Writing a book is an interesting adventure, it's a bit like inviting people into your brain to rummage around. *Look where my imagination took me. These are the kinds stories I like...*

That feeling is often intense and unforgettable. And mostly, a ton of fun.

With that in mind—thank you again for reading my work. I don't have the backing or the advertising dollars of big publishing, but hopefully I have something better… readers who like the same kind of stories I do. If you are one of them, please share with your friends and consider helping out by doing one (or all) of these quick things:

1. Visit my Review Page and write a 30 second review (even short ones make a big difference).

(http://britneyking.com/aint-too-proud-to-beg-for-reviews/)

Many readers don't realize what a difference reviews make but they make ALL the difference.

2. Drop me an email and let me know you left a review. This way I can enter you into my monthly drawing for signed paperback copies.

(britney@britneyking.com)

3. Point your psychological thriller loving friends to their free copies of my work. My favorite friends are those who introduce me to books I might like. **(http://www.britneyking.com)**

4. If you'd like to make sure you don't miss anything, to receive an email whenever I release a new title, sign up for my New Release Newsletter. **(https://britneyking.com/new-release-alerts/)**

Thanks for helping, and for reading my work. It means a lot.

Britney King
Austin, Texas
January 2018

ABOUT THE AUTHOR

Britney King lives in Austin, Texas with her husband, children, two dogs, one ridiculous cat, and a partridge in a peach tree.

When she's not wrangling the things mentioned above, she writes psychological, domestic and romantic thrillers set in suburbia.

Without a doubt, she thinks connecting with readers is the best part of this gig. You can find Britney online here:

Email: britney@britneyking.com
Web: https://britneyking.com
Facebook: https://www.facebook.com/BritneyKingAuthor
Instagram: https://www.instagram.com/britneyking_/
Twitter: https://twitter.com/BritneyKing_
Goodreads: https://bit.ly/BritneyKingGoodreads
Pinterest: https://www.pinterest.com/britneyking_/

Happy reading.

ACKNOWLEDGMENTS

A gazillion thanks to my family and friends for the endless ways you provide love and inspiration.

A thousand thanks to all of my friends in the book world. From fellow authors, to the amazing bloggers who put so much effort forth simply for the love of sharing books, to my street team and strongest supporters—naming you all would be a novel in and of itself—but I trust that you know who you are. Thank you. Seriously, you make this gig so much fun.

To my beta readers and my advance reader team... there aren't enough words to describe the gratitude I feel for you—for being my first readers and biggest cheerleaders. To Jenny Hanson and Samantha Wiley, thank you.

Last, but certainly not least, thanks to the readers. For every kind word, for simply reading... you guys are everything. Readers are always good people. Thank you for being that.

The Bedrock Series features an unlikely heroine who should have known better. Turns out, she didn't. Thus she finds herself tangled in a messy, dangerous, forbidden love story and face-to-face with a madman hell-bent on revenge. The series has been compared to Fatal Attraction, Single White Female, and Basic Instinct.

Around The Bend

Around The Bend, is a heart-pounding standalone which traces the journey of a well-to-do suburban housewife, and her life as it unravels, thanks to the secrets she keeps. If she were the only one with things she wanted to keep hidden, then maybe it wouldn't have turned out so bad. But she wasn't.

Somewhere With You | Book One

Anywhere With You | Book Two

The With You Series Box Set

The With You Series at its core is a deep love story about unlikely friends who travel the world; trying to find themselves, together and apart. Packed with drama and adventure along with a heavy dose of suspense, it has been compared to The Secret Life of Walter Mitty and Love, Rosie.

SNEAK PEEK: THE REPLACEMENT WIFE

<u>Series Praise</u>

"Clever, intense and addictive."

"Bold and in your face from the get-go."

"A twisty and edgy page-turner. The perfect psychological thriller."

"I read this novel in one sitting, captivated by the words on the page. The suspense was startling and well-done."

"Dark and complex."

"Exhilarating and suspenseful."

"A fascinating tale of marriage, secrets, and deception."

"Fast-paced and thrilling."

"A cunning tale that won't let go..."

"I haven't felt this many emotions in a book in a very long time." – Saints and Sinners Books

∼

The Replacement Wife is a riveting, powerful psychological thriller

which offers a savage look into a utopian cultish society where beauty and perfection are valued at all costs.

Statistically speaking, fifty percent of marriages end in divorce. What are the odds for murder?

Widower Tom Anderson is a savant with more affinity for numbers than people. Problem is, one is a lonely number. Thankfully, he solved for X by finding the perfect woman. It wasn't easy. Tom is very specific. He has to be.

Having checked 'find trophy wife' off his list, life was moving along swimmingly. Until that perfect woman let it slip—she has a past. One she kept hidden, almost perfectly.

Sure, she lied—she fudged the numbers. Most women do.

Now, Tom has buyers' remorse and according to cult rules only two options: get rid of her—or single-handedly erase her past.

She's a liar. But she does keep house well. And she makes a mean lasagna.

Decisions, decisions.

Razor-sharp and utterly gripping, this electrifying story explores the lengths one will go in the pursuit of perfection, little white lies that can turn lethal, and the danger lurking behind the smiles of those we trust most.

THE REPLACEMENT WIFE

BRITNEY KING

COPYRIGHT

Hot Banana Press

Cover Design by Britney King LLC

Cover Image by Nick Artnot

Copy Editing by Librum Artis Editorial Service

Proofread by Proofreading by the Page

First Edition: 2018

ISBN 13: 978-1985849839

ISBN 10: 1985849836

britneyking.com

To Melinda.
For pure chance to have been so generous and so kind...
I was surely the lucky one.

PROLOGUE

What I'm thinking is...this isn't going to end well. At least not for me. How I'm feeling is, not ready to die. What I know is, everybody's somebody's fool. And, whoever said small things don't matter, never lit a wildfire with a single match.

Let's say you are at a stop light and in the car next to you is a girl—the words 'about to die' stamped on her forehead, the word 'doomed' written all over her—and let's pretend that girl is me.

This is the opposite of a joke. This can't be real.

If only I'd known then what I know now.

Unfortunately, rumination is useless at this point. I'm on borrowed time, so I try once again to dial out. I reposition the phone. It's not working. I have half a bar, which basically amounts to no cell service. I try 9-1-1 and wait for a connection. Then I try Tom's number. No luck there either.

It's hard to save your life when you've downed half a bottle of scotch. The wine I used as a chaser didn't help.

This reminds me, I press the button for the Instalook app. Surely, out of fifty thousand followers, one of them can help me. I'll go live when the time is right. Even without service, I can record.

I clear my throat, in search of my voice.

Testing, testing, one, two, three.

God, I hope you can hear me.

I speak low and carefully into the camera. I always forget which dot I'm supposed to focus on, so I shift until I'm sure I'm front and center on the screen. I once read it's all about the eyes. I turn and shift the phone so that it's at a good angle for selfies. Beth taught me this little trick. It's a bit cramped in here and it's dark, so I'm sure if this is actually even working, it looks all *Blair Witch Project*. You're probably thinking, how do I even know this is for real? I don't know how to answer that except to say that I once saw a thing on TV about how many people witness a crime and do nothing. It's a very real thing. I know because it happened to me too. If I ever get out of here, I'll tell you all about it. For now, it's a rather long story, and I'm afraid we haven't got time for it.

Anyway, I say into the camera. My voice comes out as a whisper. Squeaky, terrified. Meek. Not like me at all. Maybe this Instalook Live thing is working. I don't know. If you can even hear me, I don't know. But if you can, listen. And if you're listening, this is the story of everything that went wrong.

Part confession. Part last rites. My final prayer.

Hear me. See me. Remember me.

I'm trapped—on my way to my final destination, my eternal resting place. And there are so many things I'd like to change but can't.

I'm going to die. In the end, all I'll ever be is just another lie on someone's lips.

This recording is...evidence. How very hopeful I was. How very stupid. So, if you can hear me—if you're listening— it wasn't supposed to end this way. Not with me in the trunk of a car, headed for God knows where. Not with me dead.

I would have gone away quietly.

It's too late for that now.

My stomach churns. Choppy waters, this business of dying.

I feel nothing. I feel everything.

You fall to your highest level of preparation, he said that once. How prophetic.

That's the problem. Well, that's one of them. I wasn't prepared. Not for this. Probably, I should have thought to stay sober. But no, one drink turned into two, which turned into… God knows how many. *Look what you've done.* I was only trying to send a message. I should have known better.

Never let them take you to a second location. I should have forced him to kill me there. It's just—I'm not ready to die. I always thought I'd be old. I thought I'd have wrinkles and saggy skin… laugh lines well earned.

You fall to your highest level of preparation. Of all of the lines he used, this is the one that sticks out the most. It taunts me, as though it could somehow help me now. My father used to say that too. Turns out, he was right. I shouldn't have let my husband skimp on our cell service. I should have argued that these things are important. Given the *one thing* that could possibly save my life says searching…searching…searching…I should have fought harder. This thing that I'm holding, this thing that's filming me. It's useless. It's basically just a holder for apps. A façade, like everything else. The illusion of safety.

My head swims.

Regret tastes horrible, in case you're wondering.

Everything hurts.

You should have stuck to the plan. I know that now.

What I don't know is, how he plans to kill me. Will it be quick? Will the liquor dull the effects? Will he make me suffer?

You never should have gotten mixed up in this. I know that too.

I can still picture the night we met, him sitting at the bar. I can still hear the music. Jazz, I think. *Focus. Only seven percent of any given message is based on the words. Thirty-eight percent comes from the tone of voice and fifty-five percent from the speaker's body language and face.*

"Have you any interest in playing a game?" he asked over his dirty martini. Funny, I can remember his expensive suit but not the expression he wore.

"Depends on the game..." I'd said with a shrug. A playful, stupid shrug. That sums up what I was—so sure of myself, so foolish in the end.

I remember he smiled. "It's a fun one," he assured me. I can't recall his tone.

He raised his finger, and the bartender placed another drink in front of me. *Researchers have found that humans have a limited capacity for keeping focus in complex, stressful situations like negotiations. Less, if there's alcohol involved.*

I remember feeling brave. That's before I knew enough to know I'm not. I cocked my head, took him in. "Unless you're on the losing end."

"Ah, a skeptic," he said. I remember he was handsome. Not spectacularly so, but enough to take notice. Not that it mattered. "Let's start with truth or dare."

I sipped my martini. His choice. I hadn't realized it wasn't a question. *When it's important, never lead with a question, always a suggestion.* "I'm going to assume you want to go first so...truth."

Another smile. "Excellent choice," he remarked. "I've always had an affinity for the truth."

You have to feel for the truth behind the camouflage; you have to note the small pauses that suggest discomfort and lies. Don't look to verify what you expect. If you do, that's what you'll find. "Most people do."

"Now that there is a lie." He shook his head slowly when he spoke. So cool. So confident. *Breadcrumbs.* "Most people only want the truth as long as it works out in their favor."

"I can't speak for most people." Maybe it was the drink. Maybe

I was just feeding him what he wanted to hear. Maybe I was just naive. It's too late to know.

That all seems like a lifetime ago. The night we met.

He toasted me. "Shall we begin?"

I lifted my brow and then my glass. "Begin away."

That's not really where it began. I know that now.

"Do you see yourself settling down?"

I almost choked. Sometimes, but not often, I was taken by surprise. *Get on the same page at the outset. You have to clearly understand the lay of the land before you consider acting within its confines. Why are you there? What do you want? What do they want? Why?* I didn't think to ask those questions. Not of myself and certainly not of him. "Settle down? You mean with a picket fence and two point five children?"

He stuck out his bottom lip, his shoulders rose to his ears. "Something like that."

I gave it some thought. My mind was already made up. "Maybe."

"*You?*" he said, eyeing my dress. "You think you could be domesticated?"

I narrowed my eyes. Classic NLP. Neuro-Linguistic Programming. I didn't know then what I know now. *Insult them at the onset; they'll work harder to prove you wrong.* "Why not me?" I scoffed. I sat up straighter, mocking him as though I was offended. Maybe a part of me was.

He touched the rim of his glass to his lips. "You don't think you're too young?"

I laughed. "My mother often reminds me that when she was my age, she was two years married and pregnant with me."

His brow lifted. "Is your mother happy?"

I gulped my martini. "She is now."

"So, you don't think most people are living a lie?"

"Meaning what?"

"In marriage. Family. You don't think it's all a show?"

"Like I said, I can't speak for most people."

He spoke directly, affirmatively. "But you think you'd be happy under such confined conditions?"

It was a leading question. I played right into it. "I think I could be, yes."

"Not a skeptic then," he decided. "An idealist."

"Is it not the truth you are seeking?"

He leaned back, away from me. *Give them space. The further they fall.* "You're good," he'd said. "I'll give you that." I waited while he glanced around the bar before turning his attention back to me. "I don't know." I watched as he drummed his fingers on the table. "Somehow, I just don't see you as the type to be content with that sort of life."

"You don't know me."

He knew me better than I thought.

"Maybe you're right. But as the Danish folk say, 'you bake with the flour you have.'" His eyes were on my legs. I remember that.

"Are you Danish?"

"No, but that's the point. You can't be what you're not."

"I'd have to be. I'm not that good of a liar."

He half-heartedly scoffed. "Oh, I'd beg to differ."

I shook my head. "I keep the emotions real. Maybe not the rest, but the way I feel, I'm not so good at hiding that."

"In that case, how about a dare?"

"Hmmm," I said, stalling. For what, I didn't know. "Those require a lot of trust." I cocked my head studying him. "I'm not sure I know you well enough for that."

"Faith," he countered. "More than trust."

"Right."

"Is that a yes?"

I smirked. "It's a maybe."

"Have dinner with me."

"Is that your dare?"

"Not exactly."

"What is it then?"

His eyes settled on mine. There was no hesitation in what he said next. "It's an invitation to make the biggest mistake of your life."

I started to tell him he had no idea how high the bar was set. Instead, I settled on, "sounds promising."

"Oh, it is."

I sipped my drink slowly, when really I felt like downing the rest of it. I asked the bartender for a glass of water. "But who would accept an offer like that?"

His expression was serious. "I was hoping you would."

I smiled, which was in effect my answer.

Now, I realize he was wrong. That invitation wasn't the biggest mistake of my life. It wasn't any of the stuff that had happened before; it wasn't trusting the wrong person, or having one too many. Not that night. And not now, either. My biggest mistake was falling in love.

You leave me no choice. I drift back to a time when I had a choice. They say the mind goes to strange places when confronted with death.

The car accelerates, and I realize we've reached the highway. There's no turning back.

Put up a fight. How? And why, if you know you can't win? Even if I could somehow run for it, I'd always be running. Sure, I could mess with the taillights, cross my fingers we'd get pulled over. I could try and locate the emergency hatch. At least this way, I will die an internet celebrity. This way my life will have meant something.

My breath comes heavier. I feel a panic attack coming on. Not that I've ever had one, but I've never cared for small, dark places.

Frantically, I search for wires. They make it look so easy in the movies. Here, in real life, it's no use. I guess you don't always get so lucky. And anyway, I'm not the captive of an amateur.

If you can't save yourself, save someone else. Leave clues like bread-crumbs. They're more likely to find you that way.

I left my clothes. Pantyhose first, panties, and at last my bra. Like a proper drunk. And now, I leave you this. I can't be sure anyone will actually see it. I can't even make a call. But Instalook says there are eighteen thousand of you geared up, in queue, waiting to watch my demise, I say, my face centered on the screen. Many more before now. Some of you, I say into the camera, maybe *most* of you, won't believe me. You may say this is fake. It doesn't matter. If believability is what you want, then I suggest sticking to the safety of the neatly colored lines of your own life. And for God's sake, if a hero is what you're looking for, let me say this up front: you're in the wrong story.

As for the rest of you, I'm going to die. I promise a good show.

∾

Learn more at: britneyking.com

Made in the USA
Lexington, KY
14 January 2019